LAURA MUIRHEAD

Copyright © Laura Muirhead
First published in Australia in 2025
by KMD Books
Waikiki, WA 6169

Cover photo © Peter Hurley

All rights reserved. No part of this book may be used or reproduced by any means, graphic, electronic, or mechanical, including photocopying, recording, taping or by any information storage retrieval system without the written permission of the copyright owner except in the case of brief quotations embodied in critical articles and reviews.

The perspective of events included in this book may be different than the perspective of others.

Because of the dynamic nature of the Internet, any web addresses or links contained in this book may have changed since publication and may no longer be vaild. The views expressed in this work are solely those of the author and do not necessarily reflect the views of the publisher and the publisher hereby disclaims any responsibility for them.

 A catalogue record for this work is available from the National Library of Australia

National Library of Australia Catalogue-in-Publication data:
Queen Code / Laura Muirhead

The best businesses have the best policies, and it's the same for people.

The Queen Code helps women lead with self-trust to rise through life's plot twists.

You are the Queen of your Queendom. My mission is to help you straighten your crown.

Part 1

FOUNDATIONS OF THE QUEEN CODE

(Themes: identity, responsibility, resilience)

Introduction
WHAT IS QUEEN CODE MASTERY™?
THE QUEEN (CENTRAL ARCHETYPE)

You might be asking yourself, "What is Queen Code Mastery™?"

A few years ago, I was having a conversation about companies having policies or guidelines on how they run their businesses. For example, when you go into a store you might see a sign on the checkout counter saying they don't do refunds, only exchanges or store credit. Banks will only cash checks for someone who has an account with them. And possibly the best example—insurance companies. They give you a policy spelling out what they will and won't cover for their insured customers.

This led me to think that we should also have policies, personal policies. These are more broadly known as boundaries, but I prefer *personal policies*. Many people bristle at the word *boundary*, and most of the time, those that do are the ones that need them the most.

Laura Muirhead

Queen Code Mastery™ is designed to help you set your own personal policies in various areas of your life—self-care and health, money and finance, relationships, where and how you spend your time, the media you consume, etc.

We do this by looking at the stories that are playing out in our lives. These could be long standing, engrained stories. Family stories, stories that started when you were a child, stories that you might believe keep you safe, stories of denial, and yes, the good stories also. Using both my signature framework of *question, investigate, heal, and grow* along with Queen Code Mastery™ Archetypes, you are able to see more clearly what your own stories are. You can decide for yourself which ones to continue with and which ones could use a rewrite.

Think of the Queen Code and your personal policies as guidelines. Just as the roads we drive have lines to help us navigate, to stay on the road—especially when unexpected curves and turns appear—your Queen Code is there to help you navigate life with clarity and more freedom. You feel more in control of your life and more secure in the decisions you make. What might surprise you is that when you set and honor your Queen Code, others in your life will honor it too!

One of the keys to Queen Code Mastery™ Archetypes working so well in your life is that *you create your own personal policies*. Because of that, they can change and grow as you do the same.

Throughout my life, I've realized that I've been able to benefit from my own personal policies, which is why I want to share some of my thoughts and lessons with you.

Chapter 1
PERSONAL RESPONSIBILITY IS A RADICAL CHOICE. THE SOVEREIGN (SELF-LEADERSHIP)

You may have heard me say this before . . .

Personal responsibility is not only a radical choice; it is empowering and freeing.

Some people like to stir the pot of drama soup with their big insufficient-information spoon then walk away from the chaos they've created.

They walk away from the hurt feelings, the broken relationships, the confusion.

Then when they are called out on their pot stirring, they play spin the bottle of blame.

Where will it land?

"Well, I thought I might have possibly seen something."

"I don't think I said *that* in the message I sent. Maybe you read it wrong."

"Someone maybe said something that I think I heard."

"It wasn't me."

And an apology? Fuhgeddaboudit!

The apology will go something like . . . "I'm sorry if you have feelings that are uncomfortable."

They won't take responsibility and apologize for what they did! Still, they point their finger at anyone or anything other than themselves.

When you make the radical choice of self-responsibility, throw out the drama soup—it's well past its expiration date—put down the big spoon, and step away from the spin the bottle blame game, you will find that there is more peace and calm in your life. Do you really need that emotional rollercoaster? Let me help you with this one . . . no.

This is where setting personal policies and creating a Queen Code come in. I created the Queen Code program to support women who are tired of the feeling of bouncing from drama to drama. (Especially when it isn't even your own drama!)

Ultimately, Queen Code Mastery™ is about being true to yourself and your core values. When you can hold your truths, your compass becomes calibrated. You may not always *know* the precise path you are taking, but you can *feel* it. If you're guided by your personal policies, unexpected doors open, and you notice the unlimited opportunities that come your way. The ones that feel aligned will be a full-on *yes*, leading you on to the next step, and the next, in the right direction.

When twists in the road show up, you will be able to navigate them with clarity, power, and grace. You will begin to see them as lessons or opportunities to grow, and you will also find gratitude in each experience.

Life is meant to be lived. It's ever-changing. And because of that, the personal policies that make up your Queen Code can shift and evolve too.

Often, those shifts come with experiences that trigger us. From what I've seen in my life, they come in a multipack, all carrying the same theme. When this happens, it's the perfect chance to use my signature Queen Code Mastery™ framework of *question, investigate, heal, and grow*.

This might look like a friend's behavior that irritates you, or by hearing a story about someone else's choices that you just cannot understand or let go of.

Here's what I do when these show up in my life. I take some time to consider where or when I've had a similar situation in the past. Many times, this can go way back to childhood days, though not always. Then, I look at it more closely: Who was involved? How did it feel at that time? Why does it still bother you when something similar comes up? Journaling is a great way to work through these questions, reflecting on your past and present feelings. The last step is to find the lesson and see where you can grow from the experience.

I'll give you an example.

One of my biggest triggers is when people are consistently late or disregard a commitment they've made. Looking closely at this for myself, I found that it traces back to multiple childhood experiences. Digging deeper, I realized it's also tied to one of my strongest core values: personal responsibility. That, along with authenticity, is right at the top of my list.

When someone doesn't follow through with their commitment, it often leaves someone else to clean up the mess. Maybe they've offered to drive you to the airport, but they cancel at the last minute. You had it checked off your list as something not to worry about, only to have to scramble at the least convenient time. Maybe a parent promises to take a child to the park, then fails to show up, leaving another adult to step in, while the child feels deeply disappointed. Or maybe it's a work colleague who drops the ball on their part of a project, leaving others to rearrange their schedules to come to the plate and cover for them.

Many times, the person who disappoints you will blame outside circumstances rather than take responsibility for overscheduling, missing details, or simply being disorganized. Don't get me wrong, life happens, and sometimes the unexpected truly can't be helped. But for some people, this becomes a pattern. It's not just disrespectful to others, it's also disrespectful to themselves.

That's a sign they need stronger personal policies. And if you allow their pattern to repeat with you, leaving you frustrated, annoyed, or drained, it's a sign that you need to tighten your own personal policies as well.

This is how the Queen Code keeps your compass calibrated, helping you to honor your values, navigate challenges, and move forward with clarity. It's not selfish to uphold your values. It's leadership. Every time you say no to what doesn't align, you create space for more of what does.

Chapter 2
FEAR IS A LIAR. THE WARRIOR QUEEN (COURAGE IN THE FACE OF FEAR)

Fear is a great storyteller . . . and a liar. I'm not talking about when you are in imminent danger. This is the lens of fear that we sometimes choose to view our lives through.

It often occurs when something unexpected happens. Something we hadn't thought of or seen coming. Something that rocks our plans or puts a fork in the road we had mapped out. Instead of taking the time to assess the situation, consider the facts, and move forward with a new plan, we allow ourselves to be thrown off balance and make assumptions without having full knowledge of the complete situation. Assumptions are a great tool to take you further down the rabbit hole of fear.

Fear allows our imagination to run wild. It creates scenarios that didn't happen and will most likely never happen. Fear makes us believe that we are experiencing or will experience terrible things. Things that are happening to us or will happen to us. Fear has us firmly living in victimhood. Fear is a liar.

Imagine this: A business owner leases space to run their business from the owner of a building. This is a very common situation. There is a lease signed for a certain amount of time. In this case a one-year contract is made between the building owner and the tenant. When that year is up, the lease ends, and they are each free to go their own way. According to the signed agreement, there is no further obligation required of either party, as long as the terms written in the lease are met.

Now, imagine that during the term of the lease agreement, the building owner, the landlord, decides to sell the building. The lease agreement spells out the right of the owner to sell, and also that the new owner will honor the existing lease with the tenant. The lease terms will be carried over to the new building owner. The lease will still end on the exact same date. The rent amount and all other agreements of the lease stay in place, only with a new owner.

Taking into consideration that the tenant may want an option to stay in the space and continue their business, the building owner, now the seller of the building, proposes that the new owner, the buyer, agrees to extend the tenant's lease. This will be made part of the terms of the building purchase. The new owner agrees. They agree to not only carry forward with the existing lease terms, but they will also add an additional six months to the tenant's lease. Six more months that were not part of the original lease.

Here's where the story gets good.

When the tenant is made aware of the sale of the building, they put on their fear glasses. The sale was unexpected. What is that going to look like for their business? Who are the new owners? How will the new relationship with them be?

These are all understandable questions. But with fear running the show, instead of calmly and logically seeking answers to their questions, the tenant starts to dig that rabbit hole, assumptions are made, and accusations are thrown at the landlord. Viewing through the lens of fear, they see themselves as a victim. They fear for the future of their business. They think the landlord conspired against them; that the landlord even withheld information of the impending sale from them during a conversation between them two weeks before the idea of the sale was even formed. They are afraid that the new owner will somehow be a threat to their belongings, and strangers will have access to their business.

I often talk about the ripple effect of positive actions. Well, here's a surprise: there is also a ripple effect of fear. The vibration of fear will ripple out to those around us. Particularly those closest to us. In this scenario, imagine a brother of this business owner who also has a business nearby in the same town. Now this brother is friends with both the seller of the building and the buyer of the building. When the brother gets wind of the impending sale, he also chooses to ride the fearcoaster along with his sibling. He chooses to see the situation through the lens of betrayal.

These friends of his have somehow conspired to betray his friendship. By deciding to go into a business deal over the purchase of a building that the brother has nothing to do with, they are betraying him. Again, assumptions are made. The integrity of both the seller and buyer is inaccurately called into question by the brother. Can you see how the rabbit hole gets bigger and deeper?

What neither one of these siblings can see is that this is a business transaction. A decision on the part of the building owner to sell the building and a decision on the part of the buyer to purchase the building. They also can't see that the seller actually considered the tenant in negotiating the agreement to sell by proposing the extension of the tenant's lease. The buyer, by agreeing to extend the lease, also considered the tenant. The tenant and the brother cannot see clearly that, because they are looking through the lenses of fear and betrayal:

The terms of the original lease have not changed; they are in the same situation with the new owner as with the previous owner.

They are actually in a better position, since they have the option to continue their business past the original end date of the lease.

All the goodwill that the original landlord has shown

to the tenant is not taken into consideration. Things like affordable rent, initial two weeks rent free, and allowing the tenant to use some of the landlord's display items and fixtures are all forgotten.

Remember the line from *You've Got Mail,* "It's not personal, it's business"? The scenario I've shared with you is exactly that. It is a business transaction. However, there are people involved, and that is what the buyer and seller took into consideration in agreeing to an extension of the tenant's lease.

This is what happens so often when unexpected situations come up in our lives. The way we react to them is so important. This is what I talk about in my book *A Funny Thing Happened on the Way to My Life*. The emotions we choose to ride in each of life's twists make all the difference. We cannot hold two thoughts at once. We can't hold two vibrations at the same time. It's not possible for positive and negative to exist in the same moment. Fear, anger, and betrayal, as you might know, are lower vibrations. If we could even arrive at acceptance, we would be in a better emotional state. If we could see the gratitude for what is happening, it would change everything. I know that isn't always easy. It's exactly why I created Queen Code Mastery™ and the Queen Code Oracle Card Deck—to help establish personal policies. When you have set policies, or guidelines for your life, it becomes easier to navigate the unexpected things that come at you sideways.

Fortunately for the owner of the building, they do have a Queen Code and solid personal policies in place to handle the inaccurate accusations thrown their way, as well as being able to see the reactions of the tenant and the brother playing out for what they are—the embodiment of the lies of fear.

This is life, there will always be change. Changes that we choose, and changes that we don't choose. It truly is how we handle them that makes all the difference. At the time, we may not see it, but often these changes end up putting us in a better place or open opportunities that we can't imagine in the moment.

> *"Only when you look back at your path will you know that every step you took was the right one"*
> *– Laura Muirhead*

My challenge to you is this: When faced with the unexpected in life, whether personal or business, take the time to calmly absorb the information and facts, and find the gratitude instead of reaching for the fear glasses.

Take action: If this resonated with you, join Laura Muirhead's newsletter. Stay connected and be the first to receive insights, inspiration, and exclusive updates!

Chapter 3
VICTIMS, VILLAINS & QUEENS

Many engaging movies have a victim in the plot line.

They also have a villain.

When you think about it, it's essential for there to be a villain in order to tell a victim story. A person, or more than one, or a thing that the victim can point to for their lot in life. Think wicked witches, weather events…maybe a tornado, or even an unexpected event like a house fire.

It doesn't have to be that dramatic though.

The stories people tell in their own lives are frequently victim stories. And when you think about it, in order to tell a really good victim story you have to have a villain. They go hand in hand.

I've witnessed it so many times.

Someone finds themselves in a situation they are not happy about.

Could be that they feel stuck, or uncomfortable where

they are at for whatever reason.

So…the easiest thing to do is point their finger at someone or something else.

Remember the Blues Brothers movie? Maybe you don't, but Jake's ex, played by Carrie Fisher, is out to get him throughout the movie. Finally, they come face to face in a tunnel. As Jake is about to meet his demise at her hands for leaving her stranded at the altar, he falls to his knees pleading…

"Honest, I ran out of gas,
I had a flat tire,
I didn't have enough money for cab fare,
my tux didn't come back from the cleaners,
an old friend come in from out of town,
someone stole my car,
there was an earthquake,
a terrible flood,
locusts,
it wasn't my fault,
I swear to Goddddd!"

Anything to avoid taking personal responsibility.
Because, here's the thing—
It was you all along. Your choices that brought you to this place. Sure, sometimes the unexpected happens, but taking a look at your choices can bring clarity to many situations.

That usually won't happen. When rooted in a victim story, people aren't looking to take responsibility for their choices; they are looking for a villain to blame their circumstances on.

Now, you might imagine a victim as someone weak, having been wronged by an unfair circumstance in their life. This is, of course, the way they view what is happening and the story they believe, and will tell.

You may have heard me talk about the stories we tell ourselves. The ones we believe, that we hold on to. In fact, this is at the very core of Queen Code Mastery™—looking at the stories we might be telling that could be keeping us stuck—and how to reframe those stories to move into more clarity and self-empowerment.

The person telling a victim story isn't ready for that. Far from it. They are interested in sharing their story far and wide. They need people to commiserate with. To take up the torch for them. To believe in them. And even take up their campaign and go to battle with them.

Remember, this is a mindset, an energy, a vibration, and a low level one at that.

When you fully believe your story and are committed to it, there is no reason for others to question that story.

So, the victim becomes a bully—railing against the villain.

I want to say right here, before we go any further, that I believe there can be three sides to a story. Yes. I said three.

Years ago I worked in an office. It was only my boss and myself there. Then, for a time, my boss's partner worked for us.

Monday mornings could be entertaining. The partner would show up and tell me about their weekend together. Frequently, it would involve a dispute or an argument they had. It would be a good story about how they had been wronged by my boss. And of course, the invitation was there to be on their side and see how they were right, and my boss was wrong. They were a victim in the story.

Later my boss would arrive to tell their version of the weekend spent together—with a twist of the story that they were right and the partner hadn't acted right towards them.

In those times I could see that each had their side, their view, their experience of what had happened. And I always felt that somewhere in the middle of those two different stories lies what actually happened.

Let's get back to our victim.

In their campaign to rally the troops around them, they tell their story to anyone who will listen. Over and over. The more they repeat it, the more real it becomes to them. People begin to believe them, even feel sorry for their mistreatment. At times these troops might even confront the villain (if it's a person—keep in mind that the villain can be a place or thing also) on behalf of the victim. They think they are being helpful and defending the poor, mistreated victim. After all, the villain has definitely done wrong—and they are out to set things right.

And because victimhood thrives on validation, this support becomes fuel.

It takes on energy.

Their voice gets louder.

They spread it to more people.

And, they add more details and assumptions, not necessarily on purpose, but because the story has begun to have a life of its own.

If the story doesn't land the way they hoped, they lean into it even more. They "go deeper." They look for proof, for allies, for justification.

They're not seeking truth, they're seeking vindication.

A person who is attached to their story will hold onto it even when it no longer matches reality. They can't see how much of themselves they're losing to it. They can't see how much damage they're causing—often to their own life, reputation, and relationships.

At some point, the assumptions collide with facts.

Reality conflicts with the story.

And everything they've been putting out there starts to unravel in their own hands.

That's when panic shows up.

They didn't expect to be challenged.

They didn't expect consequences.

They didn't expect someone to stand up to them—and hold up a mirror.

Here's the surprising thing about bullies:

They can appear strong right up until the moment someone refuses to play their game. When faced with truth, they crumble.

They stirred the drama soup with the biggest spoon they could find, and when it splashes back on them, they want no part of it.

They claim "misunderstanding," insist it was blown out of proportion, and try to walk away from the very chaos they stirred up.

They don't realize they weren't fighting a villain—they were fighting their own reflection.

They created a victim story and of course needed a villain. That villain was also created through their own story.

Imagine someone going about their own business, living their life, while assumptions are being made about what they've done. In the victim's mind, they've been targeted. Meanwhile, the supposed villain has no idea any of this is happening. They're not plotting. They're not conspiring. The victim isn't even on their radar—until the campaign against them begins.

Because when you choose to cast yourself as the victim, you automatically have to invent a villain.

If there isn't one, you'll create one. You'll assign motives, intentions, and plots. You'll fill in the blanks with assumptions, because the story demands a bad guy.

A victim story cannot exist without one.

And once the story takes hold, it becomes self-protection.

The victim will defend their narrative at all costs. They will retell it again and again, collecting sympathy, outrage, and allies. And eventually, they aren't just wounded—they are attacking.

That's when the victim becomes the bully.

Not because they're evil, but because they are desperately trying to hold on to a story where someone else is responsible for their life.

You can search for villains, or you can take responsibility—but you cannot do both at the same time.

Victimhood feels easier in the short term. It offers excuses, attention, and someone to blame.

Responsibility feels harder at first. It requires honesty, humility, and courage.

But responsibility is where your power actually lives. It gives you choices. It brings you back to the place where you are writing the story.

And that is the heart of Queen Code Mastery™:

Not denying that you've been hurt, not pretending things didn't happen, but choosing to stop telling stories that rob you of your sovereignty.

When you stop needing a villain, you stop needing to be the victim.

And what's left is the place where every true Queen stands:

Self-awareness.

Personal responsibility.

And a life written by you—not your story.

Chapter 4
SISU. THE PHOENIX (RESILIENCE, RISING AGAIN)

Have you heard of *sisu*?

"No, what is it?" you ask.

It's a Finnish word with an elusive meaning. There is no one-word direct translation to English.

Here's what you might find if you search for *sisu* on the web: "*Sisu* is an untranslatable Finnish word that implies inner strength, determination and resilience."

"*Sisu* is a Finnish term that embodies courage, perseverance, and integrity in the face of adversity."

"*Sisu* is the ultimate form of courage, the ability to persevere and not back down in the face of overwhelming adversity."

You might find it in on a T-shirt or a wall plaque artistically surrounded by words like: *bravery, spirit, courage, strength, grit, pride, tenacity, guts, determination, stamina, never quit,* or *against all odds.*

You might even say that a word that requires a conglomeration of other words attempting to describe it—and still falling short—is in a league of its own. I dare say it has its own character.

And this is what the Finnish people have. That is what *sisu* is.

I say that when you look at Finnish people, and the history of their country, they are worthy of the word *sisu*.

Finland gained independence from the Soviet Union in 1917 and survived its own turmoil of civil war in 1818. The people must endure long, cold, snowy winters with the sun maybe showing up for only six hours a day. Finns even rely on eating pickled herring, for heaven's sake—maybe on a cracker. I've even watched my grandfather eat it alone ... out of a jar. With all of this, Finland is still ranked as the happiest country in the world. The Finns are people with *sisu*.

For Finns, *sisu* is a badge of honor. *Sisu* is part of their character, their essence, their very DNA.

I say "their" but it includes me. Being half Finnish, I ca claim that I have *sisu*. It's likely not only me saying I have it, as I would guess that most people with Finnish heritage would claim *sisu*. With the variety of life experiences I've had, I suggest to you that it is *sisu* that has at least played a part in supporting me and cheering me on to continue forward despite the unexpected twists and turns of life, and to come out of each one with a lesson learned and a positive attitude to try again.

For me, *sisu* also includes a nice set of personal policies.

They go hand in hand. I don't think you can have grit, resilience, and tenacity without having a solid Queen Code to guide you.

Maybe it truly is *sisu* that is behind it all and the reason I say, "A Funny Thing Happened on the Way to My Life."

Chapter 5
THE POWER OF THE PAUSE. THE ORACLE (INTUITION, WISDOM IN WAITING)

For most of us, if we have a project or a goal we are trying to reach, it seems like the only way to get there is to keep moving forward. Even when we hit walls or spin our wheels, we think we have to try the next thing, the next option to attain the goal or complete the project.

But have you ever thought about the power of pausing? Yes, I mean taking a break from trying to push forward no matter what.

Several years ago I was trying to get a loan. It was in the middle of a divorce. I had built a horse stable a couple of years before that. There was a small house on the property—it wasn't a great house, so I planned to put a new house there for me and my kids to live in. In my mind, it would be easier to live there and continue to run my stable.

In my effort to obtain a loan I talked to a few banks and mortgage companies and even hoped to work with someone I knew who was a loan officer.

For some reason none of the options were working out. None of the mortgages were in line with my plan for my projects. I was frustrated and wasn't sure what my next step should be.

At the same time, I had committed to spending a week helping a good friend of mine. She lived in another state, and her husband was going in for back surgery. I was flying out to help her with their children so she could spend her time at the hospital with her husband.

So, I made the decision to take a pause. I took a break from searching for a new mortgage so I could focus on the task at hand—helping my friend for the week.

I didn't necessarily see it as a way forward at the time. I just knew that my frustration was too high. I didn't want to spend my time out of state thinking about or trying to find the next loan company. Or would I end up going with one of the options on the table that I didn't love?

As it turns out, after my week away, I was talking to my accountant about what was happening and hoping for another loan option. He knew people and had banking connections. In fact, he had helped me secure the loan to build my stable in the first place. He asked me if I would be open to selling the property instead of keeping it and living there.

Honestly, it was something I hadn't even thought of. I said I was open to at least entertaining the option. His suggestion was to call a well-known, successful real estate broker in the area. At that point, I felt like that broker was such a local celebrity that it wouldn't be right for me to call him. Why would he even take my call? My accountant offered to make the call for me.

A few days later that local "celebrity" real estate broker showed up at my barn. I was in the arena working with a horse. Now, he also knew horses as he owned polo horses and a polo field in our town. So, of course he was easy to talk to and down to earth. He mentioned that he might have someone who would be interested in buying my property.

Not long after that I had a purchase offer . . . and I sold the property.

Looking back, this truly was the best outcome for my children and me.

I'm not sure what life would be like if I had stayed my original course—if I hadn't taken the break from spinning my wheels trying to make something happen that didn't feel quite right. But it wasn't meant to be anyway. The universe had other plans, better plans, for me.

Ever since then I have remembered that lesson. So many times, pushing forward, making something fit, feeling frustrated, is actually the cue to stop.

When you do, you'll find in that the power of the pause. That something better, something you may not have ever imagined, will unfold in your life.

Part 2

BREAKING PATTERNS & REWRITING STORIES

(Themes: family, childhood, unspoken rules)

Chapter 6
UNWRITTEN FAMILY RULES. THE RULEBREAKER (CHALLENGING INHERITED PATTERNS)

We all want to feel important.

In the movie *The Holiday*, Kate Winslet's character realizes that she should be the leading lady in her life. We *all*, each of us, should be the star of our own lives.

When we feel we aren't getting the attention we need or deserve, this can play out in various ways.

We may tell a victim story. We may blame others for undesirable things happening in our lives. We may act up, thinking that *any* attention, even if it is negative, is worth having. This won't play out well, and you might notice that all this negativity just attracts more negativity.

This is especially true of, but not limited to, children. From the start, it's so important that a child feels loved, accepted, and important. Remember the movie *The Help*?

The young girl is told: "You is kind. You is smart. You is important."

I think so many of us didn't have that reinforcement growing up. Maybe you felt that another sibling was the star of the family. It could be for good reason because that sibling received more accolades and positive feedback from your parents. Maybe you were adopted and somehow felt like you didn't belong, instead of feeling like you were chosen to be in that particular family. Maybe you were an unexpected child and always felt unwanted. Maybe you felt overlooked or even invisible. These things can carry well into our adult lives.

All valid feelings. But can you change the story for yourself? Can you reframe it? Can you see *for yourself* that you truly are the star of your own life? That you are absolutely the most important player?

When we ourselves feel important, we don't have to take away from others. We can support and genuinely be happy for their achievements and celebrate with them. This forms an incredible positive energy that has an amazing ripple effect. Once you feel important to yourself, you are able to make others feel important, knowing that it doesn't make you any less important. What a strong sense of community you can create!

Throughout my life, I was somehow able to set goals and achieve them for my own self-gratification. At a young age, I was aware that it wasn't going to come from outside sources.

Sure, I had some adults that acknowledged certain things about me and gave me positive support, but let's just say it wasn't always the norm.

As an adult looking back, I can see that I was able to have what I call *personal policies* to guide me. This is what I call the Queen Code: a set of guidelines for life that are specifically crafted for me. They are meant to be as individual as you are, because you decide what they will be for yourself. What feels good for you. And they are not set in stone. As you grow, change, and evolve so can your personal policies—your own Queen Code.

When you are ready to take the reins of your life, to shine as the bright star that you are and be the leading lady, let's talk about how I can support you to be just that.

Growing up, we frequently take on roles in our families. As you grow, these may come to feel like labels of who you are.

Are you the star? Are you the black sheep? Are you the smartest?

So often, one sibling is favored as being the best at something. But what if you're good at that something too? It could be overlooked, and you end up feeling undervalued or left out.

Imagine if parents are always saying one of their children is bad. Does that become a self-fulfilling prophecy? You know, the child thinking, "Well, they always say I'm bad, I might as well be bad. That's what they expect."

I've mentioned before that I was never meant to be the writer in my family. That was reserved for my sister. In fact, I was never meant to be "the successful one" either. Or even smart. (All reserved, yes, for my sister.) I'm not even sure what they expected me to be—I was labeled a "Jack of all trades, master of none."

Yet here I am—an author, even an international bestselling author! And an entrepreneur, having established multiple businesses over the years: a horse stable, a bread store, and a pottery/art studio. Add to that the owner and CFO of a thriving family business.

If you find yourself in a hand-me-down family story, maybe it's time to break free of those family rules.

Sometimes it can be just as hard if you were the designated star of the family. What if you haven't measured up to that high bar that was set for you as a child?

I have seen people who have grown up being told over and over that they are the best, the shiniest star, the one meant for greatness. As children they did shine and achieve wonderful things.

When they became adults, the bar was set a little differently. Now they are living among other stars. It might not be as easy to shine so brightly, and they are normal like the rest of us.

This can be not only disappointing but devastating to the ego of the person who has been held to such a high standard for their whole life. Imagine that super star being let go from a job—maybe even from no fault of their own but because of a company downsizing. It can be crushing. I've seen it happen.

Sometimes our family expectations run so deep. It doesn't have to be that way. Our stories don't have to define who we are now. We get to choose. Sure, it's not always easy to be the unexpected successful one or the unexpected not-so-successful one. But who is defining success anyway? It's yours to define.

Ultimately, you can choose who you are, the story you are living, and the success you achieve. Measure it by your own standards and happiness. Go ahead—be bold and break those unwritten family rules! What's the saying . . . ? Something about them being meant to be broken anyway?

Remember: You are the Queen of your Queendom!

Chapter 7
MY TWO DADS. *THE NURTURER* (IDENTITY, BELONGING, CARE)

When my father passed away, his final wishes didn't include a wake and funeral. So family and friends chose to gather a few weeks later at a dinner which was not technically a wake, but a junior version of one. A fake wake.

By mutual decision, my dad and I were not on speaking terms for several years prior to his passing. In the weeks after his passing, I had been on a rollercoaster of emotions . . . angry, sad, hurt. Mostly hurt. But I finally came to an understanding that set me free from all of that.

I realized that he equated love with money. Mostly his ability to give others money made him feel loved. For the previous twenty-plus years, I didn't need any money from him. He did not see the need to give me money. So, especially in the last 10–14 years, our relationship deteriorated, aided by his need to alter history and tell my children untrue negative things about me. I had a very hard time understanding why until I put the money equation together. I guess in some strange way, it angered him that he didn't need to give me money.

As I sat at the fake wake and listened to the fond memories, I thought I would be angry. I wasn't. He financially helped so many people who thought he was wonderful for that. I knew I would sit there with a completely different perspective.

I knew I would see my stepmom, his ex-wife, who time after time while I was growing up talked about the fact that she had only one credit card to her name until my dad came along and taught her so well how to use all the credit cards. At one point, once they were separated, she told me he would buy her a diamond watch if they got back together. They did. She got the watch. Even after she financially ravaged him in their divorce, he would brag that he got off easy. Maybe in his mind that was the final show of his love for her.

And seeing her daughter—who even as a grown, married woman, and whom he rarely saw, he felt the need to make half her car payment every month—would bring to mind that in high school I made my own car payments each month without any of his help.

I often think about the fishing guide who became his close friend, and he so often helped financially. Many of dad's other friends have expressed their aggravation over just how much help he was given, though Dad chose to do it. He must have felt a lot of love from that.

When I heard his next-door neighbors talk about bringing him his mail and rewarding them each day with a dollar, I would think of my son—his grandson—who as a sophomore in high school was required to do a service project. My son sent out letters asking for donations to help build a school in South America. My dad refused to contribute, saying he gave enough money out for birthdays and Christmas. He said he couldn't afford to help his own grandson out.

As I sat there, hearing his friends a family share funny stories and warm memories, I knew that he left me out of his will. I suppose in his money equation, this was to be a cutting blow to me. It wasn't. I went to the wake not as someone who has an obligation or is indebted in any way. I was not bound by his wishes. He didn't understand that, unlike many people in his life, I just loved him for raising me, for being my dad and my kids' grandfather.

I guess he didn't understand that those neighbors' kids would have brought his mail to him without the dollar. Unfortunately, he didn't seem to know that some people will be there for you without money. He didn't know that was me.

So I realized, when we were all together on that Friday night to remember my dad, we would be remembering two very different men.

Chapter 8
SURVIVING THE WICKED STEPMOTHER. THE SHADOW QUEEN (HEALING FROM DIFFICULT ARCHETYPES)

Imagine being told that everything about you needs to change, from the way you wear your hair, to your clothes, to how you speak, or even how you express yourself.

The person who tells you this does so daily without a break.

"Girls don't dress like that."

"Girls don't talk like that."

"Girls don't like to play catch or wash the car with their dad."

Then to ice that cake, your hair is cut so you look like your stepsisters and you are told you must share all your worldly possessions with your new stepsisters.

To receive such negative conditioning as a child, you

would think it would create an unhappy adult . . . and you would be right.

However, I believe in our inherent individuality and, despite all this conditioning, it is possible to love and respect yourself just as you are and even get back to the person you were always meant to be.

It takes time, unlearning this type of negative conditioning, releasing stories that never belonged to you.

Eventually, the voice that once told you to shrink grows quieter as your own voice grows stronger.

That's the journey ... returning to your authentic self.

Like an onion, peeling away the layers of expectation, judgment, and comparison to rediscover the spark that was always in you.

Healing looks like giving that little girl a voice again. It looks like wearing what you love, speaking your truth, laughing loudly, and trusting that your way of being in the world is exactly right.

This is the essence of the Queen Code — remembering who you are before the world told you who to be.

Straighten your crown. You were never broken; you were rediscovering and stepping into your power.

When one woman remembers who she is, she gives others permission to do the same.

That's how the ripple becomes a wave — and how we rise, crown by crown.

Chapter 9
FOR MY ENTIRE LIFE—CO-CREATION. THE CO-CREATOR (MANIFESTING & SHARED CREATION)

For my entire life I've been able to attract what I am passionate about or desire . . . long before I ever heard the words *manifest* or *co-creation*.

What I have known for most of my life is that there are unlimited possibilities. I remember after graduating from high school (a year early . . . one of my "manifestations") questioning what I wanted to do next with my life. I knew that it was all up to me, and I could do anything I chose to! It would be up to me to make it happen. I also knew that I most likely wouldn't be a brain surgeon. If I really applied myself I could do it, but it wasn't something that I was inclined to do, or passionate about.

The question has always been "what do I want to do," not

"can I do it," or "is it possible."

A few of the experiences I chose to attract:

Earning my private pilot license in my twenties.

My first trip to Finland with my grandparents when I was 14.

Opening a bread store.

Building up a horse stable from a cornfield.

The time I was fortunate with the lottery.

Reconnecting with and marrying my husband after twenty-something years.

When our house burned down, we took the opportunity to have two homes in different states.

Opening an art studio.

Publishing a children's book and journals; co-authoring multiple international bestsellers; and writing my award-winning memoir, *A Funny Thing Happened on the Way to My Life.*

Training in LightWeb® and certifying as a LightWeb® Priestess.

Hosting my *A Funny Thing Happened On The Way To My Life*® podcast

Creating my signature Queen Code program, helping women to set personal policies and transform their lives.

As a Queen Money Magnet, attracted over $1.2 million dollars in what I'm calling "magic money" in two years.

All of these things didn't just happen. There was a co-creation, meaning that I had to take steps toward what I wanted, moving the desire forward and then universal energy met me in creating the desired results.

There have also been times when I realize that things weren't coming together to reach my goal in the timing or way that I had hoped. In those times, I've learned that sometimes a pause can be more valuable than trying to push things through. Sometimes that pause allows for more information to be gathered, for that "Aha!" moment to happen, or even for the universe to unfold options that hadn't been on my radar.

We create our lives moment by moment, day by day. When we choose what we really want and have personal responsibility for taking action to move our desires forward, the universe will meet us by creating magic in our lives!

Chapter 10
A FRACTURED FAIRYTALE. THE STORYTELLER (REFRAMING THE NARRATIVE)

Once upon a time there was a little girl living a fairy tale . . . only she didn't know it.

As fairy tales go, there was a fair maiden and a potential prince. They fell in love at a young age. They married and began building the empire of their dreams. A castle was acquired along with a reliable carriage. They were well on the path to establishing their royal realm, the now fair Lady and her Prince.

Along came a baby girl. The Lady and the Prince were ecstatic with the new arrival; she was the apple of their eyes and well-favored especially to the fair Lady. They were now a happy family of three.

Not long after, the Lady was attending to her royal business when she encountered an evil presence. One so dark and disorienting that it left a long-lasting mark. Even though she summoned all her strength, the evil prevailed. And nothing was ever the same again.

The Lady was shaken to her core. Distraught, ashamed, and racked with guilt, she vowed to never speak of the evil again. It had to remain her secret. The very essence of her royal realm—and that of the Prince—was at risk.

With her deep desire to put the evil in the past, the Lady slipped into deep denial. She was determined to keep her perfect royalty intact, no matter the personal cost of burying the trauma she had endured. As many do, she wove a story that would become her "reality."

Then along came another baby girl. This little Princess was not as cherished as the firstborn daughter. Though the Lady was entrenched in the story of her perfect royal realm, this Princess was a shadowy reminder of the essence of evil.

As time passed, some cracks began to tear away at the illusion of the perfection of their existence. The realm was beginning to shake. Denial ran deep, and yet, as it often does, the underlying evil essence lingered; an unseen crevice, slowly undermining the very foundation of the realm.

Eventually, the fair Lady and the Prince separated. The royal realm was torn asunder. There was a division of the estate, and of the daughters. The firstborn remained with the Lady, while the little Princess would be raised by the Prince. The happily ever after for this Lady and Prince was shattered.

Little did anyone know—well, with the exception of the

Prince—a new enchantress had caught his eye. They were quick to marry.

The Prince wasted no time in establishing a new realm. But this one was nothing like the royal fairy tale the little Princess had once known. Now, there was a wicked stepmother and two stepsisters. The rules of the realm were different, strict, unfamiliar and not up for discussion. They had to be learned, adapted to and followed.

Even though the little Princess had never been the favored daughter, she now faced a deeper level of forced conformity and constant suppression of her individuality.

It was then that the little Princess began to realize that she had, indeed, been living a fairy tale.

Time marched on. The little Princess grew into a graceful young lady. One day, after a particularly uncomfortable confrontation, and the pointed suggestion that she leave, the little Princess knew this was her chance. She fled the realm the Prince and the Enchantress built. A far-off land with new opportunities was calling, and she answered.

She was not only fleeing the land itself, but also the life and the emotional weight that had worn her down. She was hopeful, longing to reclaim her authenticity and find a sense of belonging in this new land.

Over the years, she began to do just that. She built a royal realm of her own. It wasn't always easy, finding her way, shedding the past, and growing into herself, but she persisted.

She made choices that were hers and hers alone. She learned through trial, growing with each experience, and kept going even when life got messy or hard. She was no longer the girl shaped by someone else's story. Her strength didn't come from perfection, but from persistence. And that made her a true Queen.

In time, the once little Princess had become a Queen, with a little princess and prince of her own. Her royal realm was flourishing. It was abundant, and it was hers.

Truth has a way of rising, no matter how many years it's been buried. It rises steadily until it is impossible to hold back, insisting on being seen.

And the truth that the Queen's mother had buried in deep denial so very long ago came knocking . . . right at the gates of the Queen's royal realm. It was uninvited but impossible for the Queen to ignore.

Once the door of truth had been cracked open, even slightly, the Queen could no longer look away. Her life story, the fairy tale she had lived, now called for questions. A thorough investigation was needed, reaching back to the very beginning of time, to where the story all began.

The Queen soon discovered this inquest was not for the faint of heart. Once denial is firmly rooted, it is not easily dug up. And in this case, the cover-up had been four decades in the making. Unravelling it would require every ounce of patience she possessed. Every tool she had gathered over the years. Everything she had learned about standing up for herself, and every single one of her personal policies, would be called on to unearth the truth of this misdirected fairy tale.

Indeed, it took another seven years of steady persistence to finally arrive at the truth. Question after question was met with more denial, sometimes even anger and accusations from the Queen's mother. But instead of derailing her, this resistance only fueled the Queen's resolve. She dug deeper. She investigated further.

Then, one fateful day, the Queen was able to speak to a valuable servant from her mother's court. And at last, what the Queen had only suspected for so many years was confirmed. The final piece of the puzzle had been placed.

Even as that final piece settled into place, it opened the door to more questions, forcing the Queen to reconcile the truth with the story she had been told and always believed. The fairy tale was crumbling.

The weight of the truth was heavy. For weeks, she walked the halls of her realm in silence, unsure of what she felt—relief, anger, grief. Sometimes, all at once. The story she had clung to for decades had shattered, and in its place was a stillness. But somehow within the silence, she began to hear something else: her own voice.

And now, the next step was clear.

Healing.

Healing is known to be uncomfortable for many, and this was especially the case for the Queen.

The evil presence from long ago could no longer be ignored. Her mother may have found a way to bury it, but the Queen could not. It had to be faced.

And, as it turned out, that alone held many layers. There was a physical layer. A psychological layer. And the difficult emotional layer.

Alongside all of that, the Queen had to reconcile the years she had spent believing the fairy tale was real—being told time after time that it was real life. But it wasn't. And now she saw it.

She felt betrayed. She felt abandoned by those that were meant to guide and protect her.

None of this was going to be a quick fix. The Queen gathered trusted friends and wise advisors to support her on the path. One by one, she faced each challenge, working through the pain to find her own peace.

With every layer she peeled back, her confidence grew. At times, some wounds had to be revisited, some she thought had already been healed. But healing, she learned, often moves in spirals, not straight lines.

She also learned that gratitude can be found in every situation, even the most difficult and painful ones.

That realization was a turning point for her healing, opening the door for the next part of her journey—growth.

Growth, she found, comes in increments, and is best supported by steadily working on mindset and energy. This is where steps forward are taken and positive change is created. She discovered that maintaining a high vibration and positive mindset are keys to attracting opportunities and abundance into her life. The Queen learned that when she stayed true to her passions, trusted her intuition, and shared her story with honesty and heart, magic unfolded.

The Queen was able to create solid personal policies, many she found had been quietly rooted in her since she was a little Princess. These guiding principles became her compass, what she now calls her *Queen Code*. It gives her clarity and strength to navigate any of life's twists and turns.

The real beauty of having a unique Queen Code is this: By exploring and aligning the Archetypes of the Queendom—the Villager, Knight, Servant, Princess, Queen, and Inner Sorceress—she deepened her self-love, self-trust, self-worth, and self-confidence.

These became cornerstones of her life. With those as a foundation, the Queen gained even more abundance, personal power, and intuitive strength.

And through her journey from denial to truth, from silence to sovereignty, the Queen became whole again.

And there, in the quiet of her queendom, with the sun fading and golden light spilling across the garden, the Queen no longer felt the need to protect the past. She was free. Free to rule her realm with truth, with heart, and entirely on her own terms.

The moral of this story? Life isn't always a fairy tale. And even when it seems like one, it might not be. But with clear personal policies and a solid Queen Code, you'll be better prepared for any unexpected threats to the royal realm. And when those challenges come, you'll be armed not just to defend, but to rise, rebuild, and live your own version of happily ever after.

Part 3

NAVIGATING POWER & BOUNDARIES

(Themes: self-worth, authority, saying no)

Chapter 11
THE POWER OF NOT SITTING AT THE TABLE. THE REBEL QUEEN (CHOOSING SELF OVER EXPECTATION)

While scrolling through social media, I saw a restaurant's post that said: "We're closed tomorrow. We appreciate your patience."

There was no explanation or reason given for the closure, and I was happy to see that.

Why?

Because they provided all the information that I needed to know. They will be closed. If I was planning to go there tomorrow, then I would need to make other plans. I wouldn't have to know why, that's their business. If they chose to share that information at some point, that would be up to them.

Let me ask you . . . when you read that they would be closed, did you wonder why? Did you start sorting through reasons why they might be closed?

Maybe they have broken equipment . . .

Maybe they are short staffed . . .

Maybe someone isn't well . . .

Maybe they need a day off!

Maybe none of those are true.

Here's the thing: it doesn't matter.

I created the Queen Code and personal policies based on the idea of business policies. Businesses have set rules and standards to help them operate. Those policies are to benefit the company, employees, customers, and others that they do business with. It clarifies what everyone can expect.

From my view, people should also have standards and rules—personal policies to support them in navigating life with confidence and clarity.

Do you ever find yourself (or someone you know) listing all the reasons they have for not doing something? For not going somewhere?

I hear it all the time. "I'm not going to go because . . ."

It will be too crowded.

There won't be anywhere to park.

I don't want to walk that far.

I'm just too tired.

It'll be too hot, too cold, too humid, it might rain, or snow . . . or the moon might explode.

Sometimes it's not just one excuse, but layers of them. One on top of the other; all the reasons why they have decided *not* to go.

For years, if my dad didn't want to go somewhere, he would joke, "I can't go, that's the day (or night) I'll be sorting my sock drawer." That's almost worse than the other excuses. He was so disinterested in going to the thing that sorting his socks would be more interesting. How dismissive. And yet, he still felt the need to give an excuse.

Here's a secret . . . You don't have to tell anyone why you have chosen to say no. If you wanted to go you would—end of story. It's absolutely fine to say no. And to *not* offer any excuses or reasons for your decision. You honor yourself when you say yes, or no, to the things you want, or don't want.

I want you to think about this: When you are explaining why you have decided not to do something, piling on the excuses to someone, who are you convincing? Who are the excuses actually for?

Are they to make you feel better that you aren't going to your friend's party? Are they to make your other friends more understanding? Are they listed out to help take away your guilt in the hope that you have socially acceptable reasons for saying no?

Let's go back to the "closed" post. They didn't have to offer an excuse to be closed, and neither do you!

When you have clear personal policies in place, you won't feel the need to pile on excuses, and you won't feel guilt for your decisions.

I have been to events, maybe a dinner, where everyone at the table is talking. Each person trying to get attention and to be heard. I've noticed this also happens at personal dinners. Everyone is talking and sharing, sometimes not even listening to their friends.

When I sit at those tables, listening to the conversations, yet not feeling compelled to say anything, it can make others uncomfortable. They'll ask me if something is wrong, just because I'm quietly taking in the chatter.

One time I chose to sit at the back of the room while others found their way to the front table. Spotted there in the back by another attendee, they motioned to me to move to the front of the room, offering me their seat. When I declined, saying that I was happy where I was seated, they became more insistent that I move, prompting me to again decline the offer saying I wasn't going to move from my seat.

I found it interesting that they were uncomfortable with me *not* taking a seat at the main table at the front of the room.

Have you heard the following words written by Christian D. Larson?

"To think well of yourself and proclaim this fact to the world, not in loud word, but great deeds."

There is a confidence in knowing yourself, knowing where you are comfortable, and that sometimes means observing and not having a seat at the table.

A friend told me that their daughter once asked, "Do

you think a fish knows that it's wet?" My friend responded, "It definitely knows when it's *not* wet."

Of course, that's funny, but when I thought about it further, it's about comfort. A fish is comfortable when it's wet and absolutely uncomfortable when it's not. Just like the saying "They're like a fish out of water."

So I ask you, can you be comfortable not always going with the crowd to be comfortable in yourself, without excuses?

I have found myself in rooms where others show up with an agenda of their own. It can be that they are—well, to keep with the fish theme—fishing for clients. They find out one piece about you and try to fit it into what they have to offer.

One piece of who I am is CFO of our family business. At times, people hear that one thing and very quickly run with it, inviting me to attend an event or convention that they are running. Sure, it will benefit them, but will attending their event align with our business? Will it be of benefit to us as well?

In an effort to be what they consider helpful, they haven't taken enough time to find out more about me or my business. They take one piece of my puzzle and try to fit it into their own puzzle. Often, it's not a match.

This is where it is beneficial, again, to have a Queen Code. To have the clarity and confidence to not jump into every offer from every coach that sounds like it might possibly boost your business. Know yourself. Know the team that you have in place and don't grab at every shiny object dangled in front of you.

I've had people who have too quickly extended an invitation only to discover more pieces of my puzzle. They can be surprised by how many pieces there actually are in my life. Fortunately, at this stage in my life, I have solid personal policies and a Queen Code, so I know when to say yes and when to say no. I recognize what feels aligned for me and what doesn't.

There's one more thing I'd like to share with you.

When my children were growing up, and at times misbehaving, I would tell them that there are different ways to get attention. There is both positive and negative attention, and that it's much nicer to get positive attention.

So often I see people going for what I consider the least desirable of the two. It's in the way that they show up late or disrupt the flow of things. Sure, they get attention for it, but I'm not sure they are even aware of how it can be disrespectful or even annoying. They may see it as seeming important, busy, or powerful.

For years someone I know would not answer the phone but rather let the call go to their answering machine. (Remember answering machines?) Then they wouldn't return the call for a day, or maybe more. Often by the time they called back, whatever I called about was irrelevant. It wasn't just my calls; it was family and friends. When they did respond, there would be stories of how busy they have been.

This is when I learned that being busy isn't unique. It doesn't make you special. They thought they were in control and had power over the situation. What was happening, in reality, was they were being talked about for how annoying their behavior was. It's important to have enough self-awareness to know how you're showing up. Is it with real confidence and self-empowerment, or could your actions unintentionally be disrespectful and put others off?

Here's my invitation to you: stop justifying yourself. Stop piling on excuses to cushion your "no." Let your decisions stand. You don't need a reason, an explanation, or even a seat at the table to validate your choices. True confidence is trusting yourself enough to know where you belong—at the table, in the back row, or not in the room at all. And the funny thing? The moment you stop trying to convince others, or yourself, is the moment you step fully into your own authority.

Closed. No excuse. No apology. Just a decision. That's power. That's Queen Code Mastery.

Chapter 12
FENCES AND GATES. *THE GUARDIAN* (BOUNDARIES & PROTECTION)

I've been told that I'm not always the most open and welcoming person. I don't disagree.

Because sometimes we put up fences based on what we've experienced. It can look like:

The ones that said they would protect you throw you to the wolves.

The very people you expect to care for and support you abandon you.

You've been labeled selfish just for wanting others to respect your belongings.

Telling the truth has resulted in punishment and/or abuse.

Deception has been disguised as love.

Trust that has been betrayed.

Those that were there to guide your personal development

instead undermined your sense of self and individuality.

Personal belongings that you loved or cherished were taken from you under the guise of fairness.

It's understandable, right, that you might not be open to letting people into your close circle when you've had life experiences like these. It can be difficult to hold on to your authentic self. You might think you're even losing that.

And yet somehow there's something in each of us that moves forward. That holds on to the core being of who you are. It can take the radical choice of personal responsibility to peel the onion layers. To shed the skin of who you've been told you should be and let the real you shine through.

Do you find yourself guarding yourself and who you let into your circle? I do. And that's OK. It's OK to have personal policies around relationships.

It feels like with each experience you add another post to your fence. But fences also have gates. We get to choose our gates and who we open them for.

Even though I've been told I'm not always the most welcoming to others, I can, however, be the exact opposite around people who I feel safe with. They will get my full love, support, and generosity. And they don't have to necessarily be the people I've known the longest.

I do want to add here that over the years this hasn't been the case. There have been times when I thought the people I was connecting with would be on the safe list. Turns out a few of them weren't. I allowed myself to be taken advantage of and hurt . . . fully accepting my participation in those storylines.

When I recently found myself guided by my intuition to join a group of women with a global mission, it was such a supportive, genuine experience. In fact, I found myself instantly "clicking" with a few of them.

These are the times that I'm especially happy that I've looked at and worked through so many of my past experiences. I have reframed some of the stories I was telling myself, and have my own Queen Code supported by my personal policies.

Chapter 13
BUSINESS LESSONS QC. THE STRATEGIST (WISDOM IN LEADERSHIP)

Nobody starts a business with the intention of failing.

When I decided to create my first business, a bread store, it was with great hope and anticipation. There was a lot to learn. I knew I couldn't do it on my own, so I partnered with my best friend and her husband. Each of us brought unique skills to the table and it seemed like a winning combination.

Little did we know that the business model we were using was flawed from the start since the franchisor was less than transparent and honest with us.

I still remember my nervousness as I entered the Chicago high-rise and went up the elevator to meet our potential landlord. It felt like being in a very adult world that I hadn't experienced before.

We did secure a lease, and a lawyer, and an accountant.

We bought all the right equipment and thought we were doing all the right things.

And yet it didn't work out.

It was a devastating time for me. I was blamed for the failure; after all, it was my idea and I was determined to make it happen.

People would tell me that there is something good in everything. It definitely didn't feel that way at the time. Over the years I have come to accept that it was a learning experience, but I am still sad about the loss of my close friendship because of it.

Not long after that, I had a deep desire to have my own horse stable. There was a real argument within myself because of my previous business loss. Eventually my passion won.

I bought a 40-acre cornfield and hired a well-known company to build my dream. Again, there were lessons learned. Banking and finance lessons, people that took advantage and, luckily, people that were honest—loyal friends who contributed their skills and advice.

This business was a much better success than my first one, thank goodness! I'm fortunate to still have strong connections with many of the people I met along the way. I felt that much of my previous work experience was brought together in running my stable. The pieces just seemed to fit.

In order to focus more of my time on my children, the stable was sold when I divorced.

And yet every step I had previously taken added more

tools to my toolbox.

When I reconnected with my current husband, he was already a business owner. The company has been in business since 1929. It was family owned until the last member of that family passed on, leaving no direct heirs to take over. Realizing that if the company folded, he and all the other employees would be out of jobs, my husband made a tough deal to buy the company over four years. It was a tough four years as the contract was set up for him to fail. Regardless, he succeeded by the skin of his teeth in completing the purchase.

By the time I came into the picture, he had been running everything himself for several years. We realized that my financial skill set and professional experiences could compliment his hard-working, hands-on knowledge and benefit the company. I was brought in as an owner, Vice President, and CFO.

The foundation was already in place when I came on board. Over the last 15 years we've navigated ups and downs and learned to balance our personal relationship with running the business.

It's not easy for a solo business owner to bring in a partner, trust them, and accept new ideas. Luckily, over the years, I've worn him down to listen to me more. A lot more!

As I've continued to learn, grow, and change my mindset, our company has also grown exponentially. Our sales have doubled with increasing profits. I am happy to say we are having our best year yet. Seeing the results, even my old-school husband reluctantly admits that a positive mindset and energy are game changers.

We are grateful to have a hardworking, skilled team of employees that support the work we do yet acknowledge the responsibility we have to them as owners.

This year we celebrate 95 years in business and hope to leave a long legacy for future generations of our family.

In 2019 I decided I wanted a pottery studio. A space of my own where I could peacefully create ceramics. This came off the back of learning and working in a community center where, unfortunately, people didn't always act like adults.

As my skills with molding clay grew, I found myself being targeted by others. They magically made some of my pottery pieces disappear right out of the kiln. One bowl even vanished for a whole year! I was stunned when it reappeared in a place that had been searched multiple times by more than one person.

I was also verbally abused by another artist in what should have been a safe space for learning. This was the absolute last straw. I found myself unable to focus and to be creative there.

What would my own space look like? I wasn't sure. There were a few options considered, and more than one building was looked at to purchase. Ultimately, I found the place that seemed like a great fit for me in our village.

We closed on the purchase of the building on March 20,

2020. Now, you might remember, this was right on the verge of everything closing down that year. It was even questioned whether they were going to be able to get the deed filed in a timely manner. It was filed, and the building was mine.

The next few months were a bit challenging because we had planned to hire people to make some improvements. That wasn't allowed during that time, so my husband had a fresh unexpected to-do list. Things like painting and installing flooring.

A couple of years later, we would have customers ask when we opened the studio. When we responded with 2020, they would frequently ask how opening during that time was in our business plan. Truth is, it wasn't part of the plan.

But here's the thing . . . looking back it all worked out for the best. Opening in 2020, during the days of lockdowns and limited access, gave me the opportunity to grow into having a retail space. It gave me time to get comfortable in my creative pottery-making area in the back of the studio and to make pottery pieces. It allowed me to open when I was comfortable to do so, without feeling the pressure of deadlines. It also gave me time to get used to meeting and interacting with my customers, which both my husband and I enjoyed.

Just as I set an intention to open my studio, there came a time, after much thought and fence sitting, to close the studio.

I was met with many sad faces and comments from

people thinking that I was sad. Comments like, "My heart is breaking for you." My response to that? That their heart wasn't breaking for me because I wasn't sad, and my heart wasn't breaking at all. Like I say, when the decision was made to close, it was intentional, and at that point I was more than fine with it, knowing that it was time to move on to other things in my life.

As it turned out, I had a tenant show up somewhat out of nowhere to lease the space. We moved my business out and they moved in. It was a peaceful and easy energy.

When we honor our own wants and needs, and then add intention and action, the universe will meet us in co-creating what is best for us at that time.

Here's an affirmation to take with you and use as you go along:

Everything is always working out for me!

It's true . . . it is always working out.

Chapter 14
THE DRAMACOASTER. *THE ALCHEMIST* (TRANSFORMING DRAMA INTO GROWTH)

I can finally tell you . . . we're breaking up.

It's been coming for a long time, but it feels so good to finally be able to say it out loud.

Yes . . . we are done.

I am through with drama.

Especially the rollercoaster of other people's drama. They want someone to ride the rollercoaster of drama with them, but I don't like rollercoasters anyway.

Do you know what I mean? Here, let me give you an example.

I have a friend, let's call her "Mary." Well, Mary has a relative, Lisa, that she doesn't particularly enjoy spending time with. They don't keep in touch week to week or even month to month. Mary will say she doesn't even like Lisa! Maybe about twice a year, Lisa will invite Mary to meet for lunch. Mary agrees to go but when Mary tells me she's meeting Lisa for lunch, it's always, "Ugh, I'm going to lunch with Lisa on Tuesday."

Here we go . . . do you see she is already stepping on to that dramacoaster?

When I remind Mary that she could actually say "no" to lunch with Lisa, her response is, "No, I'm going to go."

Even though Mary claims to not want to see Lisa, there is a part of her that enjoys all of it. Maybe she wants to get the tea on what's happening in Lisa's world. Maybe even get some gossip to share, or even be judgy about Lisa's life.

Then after they have their lunch, Mary will want to tell me about Lisa. "Well, she hasn't changed one bit," Mary tries to lead into some gossip, hoping I'll join, but I don't buy in. Instead, I stay quiet for a moment, then quickly change the subject to something more interesting.

I've seen this play out time and time again. When you don't take that empty seat next to them and buckle in to ride their dramacoaster, it's not as much fun for them, but it's so much more peaceful for you!

Seeing the drama for what it is and being able to break up with it is a benefit of having a solid Queen Code and setting my own personal policies.

I'd love to share this with you, my Publishing a children's book and journals; co-authoring multiple international bestsellers; and writing my award-winning memoir, A Funny Thing Happened on the Way to My Life program, to help you have more peace, navigate life with greater ease, create certainty . . . to reclaim your power and step into your Queendom!

Chapter 15
WHEN IT RAINS, IT POURS. THE RESILIENT QUEEN (NAVIGATING STORMS WITH GRACE)

When it rains it pours. Trouble comes in threes. There's a dark cloud over me.

I have to say that hearing these sayings from people in the last couple of weeks caught me off guard.

You may hear them all the time, or even say them yourself, and I used to too. But I don't think them, say them, or use them anymore. I've changed—my thoughts and attitude have changed.

Sure, you can focus on what's going wrong if you want . . . a lot of people do. When you're counting "trouble coming" where do you start? Where do you stop? Is it a nonstop parade of "trouble in threes"? Does the dark cloud ever clear?

What if, instead of counting trouble, dodging the pouring rain, or looking out for that black cloud, you counted the things going right in your life? All the good things that you have? What if we try to find out what good things come in? Do they come in threes too, or half dozens, or baker's dozens?

Things will always happen in life, believe me when I say that I've experienced my share—like our house burning down—but I see them as things happening in life that we deal with. And frequently unexpected, good things can come out of the things that happen. In fact, I call it all *A Funny Thing Happened On The Way To My Life*® and even host a podcast about our life experiences. (Maybe you've heard a few episodes.)

So, what if you tried to kick these phrases to the curb and looked for the good? I'm challenging you to find at least three good things that you are grateful for every day for a week and see how things can change. Let me know what you discover.

Part 4

WEALTH, LEGACY & VISION

(Themes: abundance, opportunities, impact)

Chapter 16
RICH BEFORE THE RICHES WITH CLARITY QUESTIONS. THE VISIONARY (SEEING WEALTH BEFORE IT MANIFESTS)

If you're comfortable, I invite you to gently close your eyes. Take a breath. Let your shoulders drop. And imagine this:

You're holding a lottery ticket in your hand. You check the numbers—one by one, they match. All of them.

It's real. It's yours. You've just won $6.7 million. Not six dollars. Not sixty. Not even six thousand..

Six point seven million US dollars.

Now, notice what rises in you. How do you feel? What's the very first thing you'd do? Who would you call? And beyond that, what would change for you? *How would* you *change?*

I invite you to reopen your eyes.

In 1994, I *did* win that lottery. Sure, I was surprised, but when my numbers came up I already felt rich. Not rich in dollars—though they certainly came—but rich in *awareness*. In *intuition*. In *calmness*. In *enoughness*.

Just weeks earlier, my dad had asked me, "Would you like to win the lotto?" and I replied: "Sure . . . but I'm already happy where I am." And I meant it.

I had a comfortable home and job. I was pregnant with my second child. Life was already full.

Winning that day wasn't luck. It was alignment.

These days, it's easy to forget what truly matters. We find ourselves striving. Straining. Reaching. For the next win. The next title. The next nod of approval. We tell ourselves that once we get there, then we'll feel whole. Then we'll be enough.

We quietly carry this belief: *If I could just win the lottery, everything would fall into place.*

But here's the truth, from someone who has been there: External wealth without inner wealth is just emptiness. All the outer success in the world can't fill an inner void. Because what truly sustains us can't be seen on a bank statement.

Yes, I won the lottery. And yet, when I go places, I don't arrive by private jet. I don't book the penthouse. I don't wear flashy diamonds or live in excess. Well, maybe a few diamonds.

Because the truth is, winning the lotto didn't change me. It confirmed me.

I know from personal experience and from working with

women around the world that wealth isn't something you have to chase. It's something you can begin to access today. When you change how success feels, you can change how you magnetize it.

You just need to understand and embrace the **eight currencies of inner wealth**.

Let's go through them now.

The first currency of inner wealth is **awareness**.

When we're rich in awareness, we're present to ourselves, to our thoughts, to what's really going on beneath the surface. We catch the stories we've been telling ourselves. We begin to respond, rather than react. Because the truth is that *not choosing* is still a *choice*.

Awareness brings us back to ourselves so we can attract the things that are meant for us with clarity, rather than from habit, fear, or noise. It's the quiet foundation on which all other forms of inner wealth can grow.

Ask yourself, what are you choosing right now? And how can you choose again so that you are in **alignment**?

The wealthiest women I know move through the world with grounded certainty. They seek wisdom. They stay open. But ultimately—they trust themselves.

I remember deciding what to do with a building I owned. Should I sell it . . . or lease it? There was a generous offer on the table. But something in me paused.

So, I followed my **intuition**. The quiet nudge that said: *Choose alignment over urgency.*

Six months later, the offer came back—even better this time. And without hesitation, I said yes. That's what intuition does. It doesn't shout. It gently leads. And that's why it's the second currency of inner wealth.

Where might you be blocking wealth simply by overriding what you already know?

One of the quiet mistakes I see is acting from desperation. Not because we've failed, but because we've been taught that urgency is power, that rushing means progress.

But desperation has a frequency. It clings. It pushes. It grasps. And when we move from that energy, we chase what was never meant for us. We say yes too quickly. We hold on too tightly.

Desperation repels. But **calmness**? Calm is magnetic. Calm says: *What's mine is already on its way. I don't need to prove or push.*

So, take a moment. Think of something you deeply want. And ask yourself: *If I already knew it was coming, what would I do differently today?*

Would you slow down? Breathe more deeply? Let yourself enjoy the in-between? Because when you move from calm, you align with what's meant for you.

Calm doesn't chase. It calls. And that makes it the third currency of inner wealth.

When I bought the winning lottery ticket, I didn't check it straight away. Not because I forgot—but because I wasn't chasing it. I wasn't waiting for it to prove anything. I already felt rich. Whole. Enough.

The win didn't complete me. It confirmed what was already true. And that's the part so many of us miss: You're not worthy because of what you've achieved or what you own.

You're worthy because you're *you*.

Not because of titles or income. But because of something deeper. Something quieter. Something that's always been there. **Enoughness** is the fourth currency of inner wealth.

So, here's a gentle invitation to come home to yourself. Complete this sentence without using any titles or achievements: "I am enough because . . ."

Let the words rise. Let them come from the part of you that doesn't need to prove anything. Because when you believe this not just in your mind, but in your being, the richest life you can imagine begins to unfold. Not because you've earned it. But because you've finally made space to receive it.

That's the power of inner wealth.

The fifth currency of inner wealth is **embodiment**.

For years, I put off writing my memoir *A Funny Thing Happened on the Way to My Life*. The stories were there, but something in me kept holding back—as if I needed permission.

Then one day, I saw my face on a billboard in Times Square. And it struck me. This happened because I started showing up as the woman I was becoming before the world caught up.

That's embodiment. It's not about pretending. It's about choosing to show up as if you're already there.

So, let me ask you: Where are you still waiting for permission? And what if the version of you who already had it all . . . didn't wait?

The sixth currency is **alignment.**

When I was 12, I decided I wanted to visit family in Finland. So, I started saving my babysitting income, birthday money, and holiday gifts. By 14, I'd saved enough to go.

Later, I set my sights on earning my pilot's license. And I made that happen too. Not because it was easy, or because I had it all figured out—but because I was clear on what mattered and moved in line with that.

Money alone doesn't fix misalignment. You can have plenty of money and still feel lost.

But alignment? That's where magnetism lives. When your values and actions sync up, things begin to flow. Not always quickly—but deeply.

So, set aside the "shoulds" and ask yourself: What truly matters to you?

The seventh currency of inner wealth is **gratitude**.

Let me take you back to the moment I found out I'd won the lottery. What I remember most wasn't the money—it was the reactions.

Some people became distant; others, unexpectedly, entitled. But a few? Their eyes lit up with genuine joy. Not because they were getting anything, but because they were truly happy themselves. And had space to be happy for me too.

Those people were already rich. Rich in gratitude.

Because gratitude isn't about pretending life is perfect. It's about noticing what's already working—even before the miracle arrives.

So let me ask you: How did you feel when you read I'd won the lottery? Did something in you expand? Or did it contract? Did a flicker of envy arise? Did something shift in how you saw me?

Whatever came up—just notice. It could be telling you about your own gratitude. After all, a rich and grateful heart is already full.

The eighth currency of inner wealth is **community**.

Because true wealth isn't built alone—it's built through connection. But not just any connection. The right people matter. Those who see you. Who honor and serve your energy. Who meet you on your frequency.

Our wealth moves in circles—through shared values, trust, and reciprocity.

Years ago, I dreamed of building a horse stable. I hit every wall—until one man, the president of a bank, heard my story and quietly opened a door. Years later, I stood on the other side congratulating a graduate who had retrained as an electrician. We gifted him tools to begin his new path.

That's what an aligned community does. It gives without

Queen Code

an agenda. And receives without guilt.

But here's the truth: You get to choose who you give to—and who you receive from.

This isn't about being closed. It's about being intentional. Not everyone is meant to walk beside you. And that's OK.

So, reflect on your circle. Who lifts you? Who drains you? Who truly meets you where you are? Because when you surround yourself with the right people, you don't just feel connected—you get richer.

- Awareness
- Intuition
- Embodiment
- Calmness
- Alignment
- Enoughness
- Gratitude
- Community

These are the currencies you can access to shift from chasing to claiming.

Now, I invite you to gently close your eyes . . . again. Let your feet settle on the floor. Let your shoulders soften. Let your breath slow.

You've just moved through eight currencies of inner wealth, each one a quiet reminder that you are already enough. Already whole. Already rich.

Now, bring to mind the richest version of you. The one who isn't waiting. Isn't proving. Just *is*—complete and grounded.

She's not far away. She's in the room with you. She's in *you*.

And gently ask yourself: What is she ready to release? What is she open to receiving? And what is she deeply grateful for?

Chapter 17
THE BUFFET. *THE EXPLORER* (CHOICES, TASTING LIFE'S OPTIONS)

For Christmas my husband was gifted an infuser.
The Cambridge Dictionary definition of infuse:
verb: to cause someone or something to take in and be filled with a quality or a condition of mind

The idea with this particular infuser is to combine oils, herbs, fruit and/or sugar to make oils, syrups, or flavorful bases for beverages. The essences of each ingredient merge together to make a single delicious flavor that is more enhanced than each of its parts.

As I thought about the concept of infusion, it came to me that this is a beautiful metaphor for life and what we can do for ourselves. Just like we select each ingredient for a recipe, we can mindfully choose the thoughts, ideas, intentions, emotions, and habits that will shape our life experiences, not only today but also for who we want to become.

Imagine creating your life as an infusion: combining ingredients like the freshness of good thoughts, the grounding of clear intentions, the sweetness of gratitude are all important. Blending these "ingredients" creates a delicious essence to flavor who we are and how we experience in life.

At the same time, adding the wrong ingredients—negativity, worry, or fear—can spoil the batch.

So, here's the question: What ingredients are you adding to your infusion today? Are they supporting your happiness, growth, and well-being? Or do you need to adjust the recipe?

Let's try another metaphor.

Imagine you pick up a plate at the beginning of a buffet line. You hold your plate, excited as you look over all the choices. But instead of food, laid out in front of you are choices. Choices of life experiences, emotions, relationships, and energies.

Which ones will you place on your plate and what will you pass on? Will your plate be balanced?

What do you do if someone tries to add to your plate? To load up your plate with their choices? Or judge what you've put on your plate? Maybe they'd like to take something from yours that you're not willing to give them.

I love the saying, "Keep your eyes on your own plate." Would you be willing to say that to someone? Are you able to do that for yourself? To not judge, take away, or add to someone else's plate?

Queen Code

Maybe it's time to clear your plate, having enjoyed what has been there, but you're ready to make room for fresh, new experiences, relationships, and choices.

Here we are with all these choices in life. With a plate we can pile high! Sometimes it's hard to remember that we are the ones that get to choose what we want. How we feel, what we create in our lives.

How will you fill up your plate?

Chapter 18
DREAMS COME TRUE (NOT THE WRITER). THE DREAMWEAVER (MANIFESTATION)

Dreams that I didn't know I had came true!

Having my book *A Funny Thing Happened on the Way to My Life* broadcast on a Times Square billboard is something I never imagined. Through my whole life, I never even thought of being on a billboard in Times Square. And yet there it was . . . *there I was* . . . in the middle of Times Square, New York City, surrounded by family and friends, celebrating exactly that.

In fact, younger me wouldn't have imagined being the author of my own book because I was never meant to be the writer.

You know how families go. Setting up ideas for what the future of each child looks like. Well, I was never meant to be the writer in my family. That was reserved for my sister.

In fact, I was never meant to be the "successful one" either. Or even smart. (All reserved, yes, for my sister.) Not even sure what they expected me to be, being labeled a "Jack of all trades, master of none."

I think of a time when our report cards came home. I can remember the gushing of how my older sister had straight As. Amazing, right? Something to be celebrated for sure. What confused me was why, with all As and only one B on my report card, that was not acknowledged or celebrated.

It was always understood that I was expected to get good grades. The support and help from my parents weren't necessarily there to achieve that. Imagine my frustration when I was young and asked my dad to help me spell the word "orange." He told me to look it up in the dictionary. Wouldn't I need to know how to spell it to look it up?

At Christmas time my mom and sister were happily wrapping and decorating presents. I asked to help but was met with an air of "you can't do it right." Even though I was shown how to wrap them, surprise, my wrapping didn't meet their standards.

My family bought a piano so that my sister could take piano lessons. The only time I was allowed to touch it was for a photo my mom took of the two of us sitting there on the piano bench. Years later, Gene and his second wife bought a piano. This time I had no choice but to take lessons and learn to play. I was in the school band playing the clarinet, having started playing the cornet in grade school and changing instruments after 6th grade.

For the most part, my parents didn't attend my school concerts or programs—maybe one or two. I got the impression it was an obligation they didn't want to be bothered with. For me it was a double-edged sword. Of course I wanted the support, but I really didn't care to have my stepmother attend.

I was really interested in taking horseback riding lessons after we had a babysitter that told me she was riding. By some sort of miracle, I was able to do that! A few months into my lessons, I was able to "borrow" a pony from someone my mom knew. I'm not sure what the details were, but I knew he was mine to ride! We were even in a horse show together. That, unfortunately, wasn't long-lasting. The decision was made during my parents' divorce that the pony had to go. Lucky for another young girl at the stable where I rode though. She was able to take the pony over. I was crushed to see it. My lessons continued for a few more months on barn horses until my stepmother put an end to horses for me altogether.

The horse passion didn't subside in me. As an adult I was able to fulfill that by riding again, eventually showing and owning my own stable that offered riding lessons and horse boarding.

I'm grateful that somehow there was always something in me that drove me to do well for *myself*. To have a desire to follow my passions—and yes, there have been a few, whether it was horses, flying airplanes, starting and running businesses, art and creativity, or, yes, writing. I have published and illustrated a children's book, a series of three journals, and have become an international best-selling author. And now the author of my own memoir, that was on a billboard . . . in Times Square.

Hold on to your dreams, put them out into the universe, and say yes to opportunities that feel aligned.

Stay tuned . . . there's more to come.

Chapter 19
THE IDEA BEFORE THE IDEA. THE MUSE (CREATIVITY SPARK)

Who do you think of when you think of someone creative? An artist? A painter? A photographer? A writer?

What about yourself?

We seem to think creativity belongs to the few, the "talented," the ones holding brushes or cameras or pens. But creativity isn't just about making art. It's about making choices.

I keep these words by Henri Matisse on my wall: *Creativity takes courage.*

Because it does. Facing a blank page, an untouched canvas, or a fresh ball of clay can feel paralyzing. That first mark, that first brushstroke, that first touch . . . it's a commitment. And that commitment can feel scarier than the blank space itself. But what's worse, really: facing the blank page, or risking that what you create won't turn out the way you hoped?

I've been there. When I worked with clay, I'd sometimes sit for a minute just holding it, wondering what I wanted to create. And as a writer, the blinking cursor on a blank screen can be just as intimidating. But I've learned that creativity flows once you simply begin. And sometimes it goes in a different direction than you originally expected. I've also learned to accept those unexpected outcomes. Many times, they end up being better than what you first intended.

I've heard so many people say, "I'm not creative." But I don't buy it. We are all creative. Every moment, ideas form in us. Some take root like seeds, growing when we nurture them. Others drift away.

One of the core principles of my Queen Code Mastery™ framework is looking at the stories we tell ourselves, and the courage it takes to rewrite them. We don't just create art; we create narratives about who we are, what's possible, and what we deserve. Sometimes those old stories limit us, holding us back. But creativity gives us a way out. Just as we can change a painting with a single brushstroke, we can begin to shape a new story for ourselves by daring to create something different.

Here's the truth: We are all creating our lives the same way art is created. What we choose to focus on, the actions we take, and the stories we choose to believe—that's what becomes our reality.

Every thought, every choice, every "yes" and every "no"

is part of the creative process. And just like facing the blank page or ball of clay, it takes courage . . . to keep shaping, to keep showing up, even when the next steps can feel uncertain.

So maybe the real question isn't, *Are you creative?* But rather, *What are you creating in your life right now?*

> **Take action**: If this spoke to you, stay connected with Laura Muirhead. Join her newsletter for more reflections on creativity, courage, and life as art, along with updates and inspiration.

This brings us to the "Idea Before the Idea."

Are unicorns non-existent because you've never seen one? Are they imaginary? You imagine them . . . so they aren't real?

I had this quote on a sign in my art studio: "Everything you can imagine is real." – Pablo Picasso

At some point, everything was a thought. An idea. Imagined.

What if Thomas Edison hadn't imagined his light bulb? What if Alexander Graham Bell hadn't imagined the telephone? What if Henry Ford hadn't imagined the Model T and the assembly line? And what if Karl Benz hadn't imagined the two-stroke engine? What if the Wright brothers hadn't imagined taking flight in an airplane? What if Steve Jobs hadn't imagined the Apple computer, the iPod, iPhone, or iPad?

None of these things would have existed if someone had

not had an idea. They had a vision. They imagined.

Then they worked on their vision. Made a plan. Tried, again and again, until it actually worked.

Alexander Graham Bell once said, "Before anything else, preparation is the key to success."

Your vision is important, but staying the course, showing up, and putting in the work? That's where the magic happens.

Let's talk about Alexander Graham Bell. I got curious and started digging into his story.

Not only did he patent the telephone, just hours before a competitor, but he also improved Thomas Edison's phonograph. His interest in working with sound and communication was personal. His mother was partially deaf, and his wife, Mabel Hubbard Bell, lost her hearing as a child—a result of scarlet fever. He was a teacher working with deaf students and was inspired to invent communication solutions for them.

You may not have heard of Mabel, but she played a big role in encouraging and supporting her husband's scientific work.

Alexander experimented with using light to transmit sound, which he called the photophone. He and a partner successfully transmitted a wireless voice message using a beam of light. This was long before fiber optics existed!

He experimented with sound recording and developed an early version of a metal detector. It was first used in an attempt to find a bullet after President James A. Garfield was shot. Even though it wasn't successful at first, that technology was eventually used in operating rooms.

Bell also explored flight, specifically testing wing and propeller blade shapes. It was Mabel who funded the Aerial Experiment Association he founded.

Alexander also took the reins as president of the National Geographic Society from his father-in-law, and later encouraged his son-in-law, as editor of National Geographic Magazine, to use more photographs and fewer articles to make the magazine more popular.

Meanwhile, Mabel made her mark, advocating for education, helping to establish the first Montessori classes in Canada, and supporting home and school associations. Through this work, she left a legacy of her own.

The Bell Telephone Company was founded in 1877.

Believe it or not, I have a connection to this story.

My dad began working at Bell Telephone as an installer, then a successful salesman, and eventually retired as a Marketing Manager, after it became Ameritech.

Of course, Alexander Graham Bell's imagination changed the world, but it also became part of my own story.

What if he had kept his ideas to himself? What if he hadn't allowed his imagination, that creative spark, to catch on? If he ignored what he saw as a need in others? Or even talked himself out of trying?

Bell believed in the power of clarity and persistence. He said:

"What this power is I cannot say; all I know is that it exists and it becomes available only when a man is in that state of mind in which he knows exactly what he wants and is fully determined not to quit until he finds it."

That's what took his ideas from a spark to something real.

Sure, maybe the telephone still would've come into existence. But would it have been the same? Would the Bells have made such a lasting impact on innovation and education? We'll never know . . . because he *did* share his vision. And we're all still feeling the ripple effects.

> "When one door closes, another opens; but we often look so long and so regretfully upon the closed door that we do not see the one which has opened for us."
> – Alexander Graham Bell

Imagination opens those doors—we just have to be willing to look.

> "Concentrate all your thoughts on the task at hand. The sun's rays do not burn until brought to a focus."
> – Alexander Graham Bell

Maybe imagination is just energy waiting to be focused.

I talk about this in my recent *Awakened Magazine* cover story; how those first hints, the idea before the idea, are at times, what lead us somewhere meaningful. In that interview, I shared how following what lights me up (even when it doesn't totally make sense yet) has led to some of the most unexpected and beautiful chapters of my life.

And what about the unicorn?

I've never seen one. Except in my imagination.

So far, anyway.

> **Take action**: If this resonated with you, join Laura Muirhead's newsletter. Stay connected and be the first to receive insights, inspiration, and exclusive updates!

Chapter 19
LIFE'S BOUNDLESS POSSIBILITIES. THE ADVENTURER (FREEDOM, EXPANSION)

As a young child in Chicago, one of my favorite shows was *Bozo's Circus*. It was a local classic. I can still hear the announcer... "Bozo's Circus is on the air!" Cue the familiar, big top carnival music. Sometimes I was even allowed to watch the show while I ate my lunch, sitting on the floor with a TV tray.

One of the highlights of the show was The Grand Prize Game. Magic arrows randomly choose a boy and a girl from the live audience to play the game. At-home viewers could send in a postcard with their name, and each player would draw a card. With each toss of a ping pong ball into six numbered buckets, they would win prizes along with the lucky person whose postcard they chose.

Imagine my heartbreak when we moved a few hours

away and I discovered *Bozo's Circus* was not on the air in our new town! Those were the days before cable television and binge streaming shows.

A week or two after we moved, we were notified that I had been one of the lucky at-home viewers whose card was chosen and to be on the lookout for the prizes. It was amazing! Packages were delivered, each one with a new surprise. I won clothes, games, and toys. It was a great consolation for not being able to watch the show anymore.

Looking back on that time now, it was just the first of many experiences that you might call fortunate or lucky. These days, we might even call it manifesting or co-creating with the universe.

For my entire life I've been able to attract what I am passionate about or desire. When I was eight, beyond all odds, my parents said yes to my request to take horseback riding lessons.

To mention a few: there were new bikes, my first trip to Finland with my grandparents when I was fourteen, graduating a year early from high school in three years, and moving to California at eighteen. I earned my private pilot license in my twenties, opened a bread store, and built up a horse stable from a cornfield. There was the time I was fortunate with the lottery. After twenty-something years I reconnected with and married my husband. After our house burned down, we took the opportunity to have two homes in different states and then open an art studio. I have also published books, meditations, and created my signature Queen Code Mastery™ program and companion Queen Code Oracle Card Deck, helping women to set personal policies and transform their lives.

What I have known for most of my life is that there are unlimited possibilities. I remember, after graduating from high school, questioning what I wanted to do next in my life. I knew that it was all up to me . . . and I could do anything I chose! It would be up to me to make it happen. I also knew that I most likely wouldn't be a brain surgeon. If I really applied myself, I could do it, but it wasn't something that I was inclined to do or passionate about.

The question has always been "what do I want to do," not "can I do it," or "is it possible."

All of these things didn't just happen. There was a co-creation, as I mentioned, meaning that I had to take steps toward what I wanted. To move the desire forward. The simplest example of that is sending in a postcard with my name on it to *Bozo's Circus*. There was no way to win if I hadn't taken that basic step.

There have also been times when I realized that things weren't coming together to reach my goal. In those times, I learned that sometimes a pause can be more valuable than trying to push things through. Maybe that pause allows for more information to be gathered, for that "Aha!" moment to happen, or even for the universe to unfold options that hadn't been on my radar.

We create our lives moment by moment, day by day. When we are able to choose what we really want and have personal responsibility for taking action to move our desires forward, the universe will meet us in creating magic in our lives!

Over time, I began to notice a pattern. Whenever I followed what sparked curiosity or excitement, opportunities appeared—usually in ways I couldn't have planned. It wasn't about having every detail figured out, it was about saying yes to the pull of possibility. That energy of adventure has always guided me more than any carefully mapped plan ever could.

Looking back, that Bozo's Circus postcard taught me more than I realized, it showed me that magic (the universe) meets us halfway. I had to send the card before anything could happen. That lesson has followed me ever since… take the step, then trust the unfolding. Some paths move quickly, others take more patience, but each has its own timing.

Say yes to the call, take the step, and trust the unfolding. That's how The Adventurer creates her world…one brave choice at a time.

Part 5

LESSONS IN IDENTITY & SELF-MASTERY

(Themes: growth, alignment, authenticity)

Chapter 20
WHAT IF . . . THE VISIONARY DREAMER (POSSIBILITY THINKING)

What if the key to it all is owning your truth? Telling your whole story.

Not denying or suppressing parts that you think should stay hidden because you think they are shameful, or you feel guilty about them.

What if telling your story not only heals you but also heals others, or maybe even more importantly saves and/or protects others?

What if that's the key to your body feeling whole—your abundance flowing, opportunities cracking wide open?

What if you can let go of the part where you think you were somehow to blame or feel responsible for the actions of others? Or that somehow a bad seed was passed down and also planted in you? That the coincidence of shared DNA makes you like *them*. What if you stopped trying to dig up that seed and just be you?

What if being your authentic self, telling your story and owning your truth is the magic you've been waiting for and searching for all along?

The key to all the locks. The magnet for golden opportunities. The path to unfolding your dream journey.

What if that is what created the ripples that become waves of inspiration for others?

What if you finally getting out of your own way, taking personal responsibility and telling your stories, makes you whole, gives you confidence, and most importantly brings you peace?

What if you shining bright is the beacon that lights the way for someone else?

Chapter 21
WHAT DOES A PEANUT BUTTER SANDWICH HAVE TO DO WITH IT? THE INNOCENT (SIMPLICITY, PLAYFULNESS)

What does a peanut butter and jelly sandwich have to do with Queen Code Mastery™?

Everything!

When people say they don't like having boundaries, I like to talk about a PB&J sandwich.

Think about it . . . when you are making a sandwich, what are you using? Do you like white bread, wheat, rye, sourdough, or cinnamon raisin bread?

Most likely if you are making a PB&J, you won't choose cinnamon bread. Or who knows . . . maybe you will.

What about the peanut butter? Do you use creamy, chunky, or even a certain brand of peanut butter? Is there a brand that you absolutely won't buy or want to eat?

Now the jelly. Is there a flavor you prefer? Jam, jelly, marmalade? Again, do you have a favorite or are you pretty open to any of them?

My great-aunt would make raspberry jelly. Homemade raspberry jelly on a peanut butter and jelly sandwich in my school lunch was the best!

How much peanut butter are you going to put on the bread? On both slices or just one? How much jelly do you like? So many things to consider.

I know that my husband only wants white bread. He prefers strawberry jam and creamy peanut butter. For me, I definitely have a brand of peanut butter that I prefer.

So back to the question: What does this have to do with Queen Code Mastery™?

Everything, because this is a great example of personal policies.

When making a sandwich, you might have a hard no on some of the ingredients, and some of them you might be more flexible about. It's the same with your Queen Code and personal policies. That's the beauty of it. You create personal policies that feel good to you. Some will be a hard no. Others will be a bit flexible. But they all will be tailored to you and what feels good for you in your life. Just like when you sit down to eat that perfect sandwich you made ... delicious!

Chapter 22
CRISIS TO CRISIS. THE SURVIVOR (NAVIGATING CHAOS)

Do you ever notice how some people seem to bounce from crisis to crisis in their life? They often thrive on the attention it brings, telling a story that the universe is against them, or that someone has wronged them. Looking for emotional or financial support . . . thinking that any attention, even if it's negative, is worth having.

You might also notice that they rarely take personal responsibility for what's happening in their life. These are solid, believable stories—but they are just that: stories. That's why it's so important to understand the Archetypes of Queen Code Mastery™ and recognize how they look and feel, both when aligned and unaligned.

When we connect with the Queen Code Mastery™ Archetypes, we can step out of victimhood and into empowerment. Each Archetype holds a unique energy, and when we learn to recognize the signs of misalignment, we can begin to shift our focus from seeking external validation to embracing our internal power.

This work helps us to see our life experiences through a new lens—one that invites responsibility, growth, and the ability to create rather than react. When aligned, the Queen Code Mastery™ Archetypes guide us to lead with purpose, resilience, and grace, making us less likely to fall into cycles of chaos or drama.

Instead of being caught up in crises, we can embody calm, centered, and confident energy, attracting the right kind of support and thriving without needing to seek attention in negative ways.

Curious about how to align with these Archetypes and bring more balance into your life? Stay tuned for more insights on how to activate your Queen Code and step into your true power!

Chapter 23
GOING FROM PASSION TO PASSION. THE SEEKER (LIFELONG GROWTH)

The societal norm has been: choose one thing, one path, one passion at a young age (18 or 20) and stick with that for life. Choose at an age when you don't have a ton of life experiences (comparatively). Don't change what you've chosen to do, or you will seem flakey or unreliable. Even being told you won't have a decent retirement package moving from job to job.

Years ago, the path to success was to work for one company, move up within that company, and stay until you retire with a good pension. At times, that required physical moves to other cities to gain a promotion.

Some people weren't willing to move—so no promotion—but still would end up with a decent retirement package. I've seen people, who are unwilling to change, criticize and judge the people who would move to take the promotion opportunity.

What is this mindset? The idea that it's bad or wrong to move or change jobs? Is it our tribal mentality that it's not safe to leave the safety of the core group? To stay stagnant and not move or think "outside the box"!

For those of us who have worn many hats, followed our hearts from passion to passion, we have accepted the ups and downs—*experienced the perceived failures*—and took those as lessons for growth and accepted the new experience journey that would come from that.

Throughout history, the people who changed the world didn't follow the prescribed path—they followed curiosity. Some of the innovators we celebrate today—like Steve Jobs, Clifford Holland (the engineer behind the Holland Tunnel connecting New York and New Jersey), Amelia Earhart, Charles Lindbergh, and Sir Richard Branson—each took bold ideas and turned them into reality. Their willingness to take risks and think differently paved the way for what we now consider progress.

I personally have gone from passion to passion following my heart and intuition. It has served me well and given me a toolbox full of experiences and knowledge to share with and support others.

From starting and running businesses from scratch (literally building a horse stable from a cornfield) to piloting airplanes, multiple real estate transactions, both residential and commercial, an art studio, bread store, and CFO of our family ship-repair business.

I've lived in places ranging from the Midwest to both the West and East Coast of America, and I have traveled to many countries around the world, soaking up the variety of cultures each location offers.

My life hasn't followed a straight, anticipated trajectory. The path has been filled with unexpected twists and turns. That's why I say affirmatively: I wouldn't have it any other way.

Chapter 24
YOU ARE THE CAPTAIN. THE NAVIGATOR (SELF-MASTERY, DIRECTION)

"You are the captain of your own ship; don't let anyone else take the wheel."

– Michael Josephson

Do you believe that you are in control of your health? It seems that we go along, day to day, *hoping* that we don't get any number of diseases. Just *hoping* that something won't happen. What if you knew that there are things that you can do, starting today, starting *right now*, that you can do to help your body steer toward feeling better? Would you do it? Would you take control of your own well-being in an effort to at least raise the odds of your body being well? *And* lowering the odds of something happening?

Yesterday, my husband and I stopped at a gas station/mini-mart. The parking lot was full—I'm not talking about the gas pumps—the parking spaces to go into the store were full. It hit me that there are so many people stopping at places like this every day to get coffee, fountain drinks, snacks, cigarettes, candy, etc. I know for a fact there is one such location in a small town grossing over four million dollars a year. This is what we are putting into our bodies—in a huge way! We grab a quick snack of delicious chocolate-flavored processed sugar rolled together with some chemicals and wash it down with a sugary processed drink. Think for a minute about how this could be providing our bodies with anything they need to function properly. Have you thought about if, in fact, these types of foods might not only be *not* providing nutrition, but might also be detrimental to your body staying well?

If you can just adjust your thinking about what is going into, on, and around your body, then you are taking the first step to helping it feel better. If you can just make conscious choices, small changes, each day about what you eat, then you will begin to give your body what it needs to actually get stronger in fighting sicknesses versus making it weaker and more susceptible to them.

Unfortunately, so many of the things we now eat contain chemicals that our bodies just can't deal with. Take a minute to think about all the ingredients in some of the foods you've eaten today. We have been told for so long that all of these things are OK to eat that we accept that they *are*. We have come to believe that eating that way is not only OK, but also actually cheaper than eating real food or using natural tools to support our well-being.

Let's think about that. Think about whether what you've been eating has been working for you. *Has* it been working for you? Do you feel good? Do you have energy? Do you sleep well? Have you been spending time in the doctor's office? How much? How much is that costing you?

Here's why I ask. It's important to me that you know there are things you can do to be the captain of your ship. To steer your vessel in the direction of feeling good. Of feeling less pain. To spend less money on things that are not helping your body in any way to be well.

I ask because four years ago I felt terrible. There were so many ways I felt bad that I didn't even realize it until I felt better, which took a little time. Every time I thought I was feeling as good as I was going to feel, a couple weeks would go by, and I would feel even better. I'm not going to lie, it didn't happen overnight, but we didn't get our bodies in the state they are today, feeling crappy, overnight. It's been a learning and growing experience, and it has taken commitment. I am committed to *myself*. It's *important* to me that I feel good and that I do everything I can to give my body the opportunity to be well. To hedge the bet against sickness. To not only *hope* that my body will remain well, but to give myself a solid foundation for that hope.

Remember in the movie *Freaky Friday* when Jamie Lee Curtis drops Lindsay Lohan off at school and yells, "Make good choices"? Well, that's my challenge to you . . . to make good choices. Make conscious choices of what you eat. Think about it. Would it really be so hard to choose an apple over a Ding Dong? It's just making small changes, and then making them more frequently. Pretty soon, they will be *easy* choices.

How long has it been since you've felt good? Can you remember when that was? What if you just tried this for a few weeks? What's the worst that could happen? If you don't feel better, you can always go back to eating the way you always have. But what if you do feel good? Ahhh, wouldn't that be great? Give it a try and let me know what happens.

How Far Can You Hear?

Sometimes, in the quiet of the morning, before I even open my eyes, thoughts run through my head. They might be about the things I need to remember to do that day.

Does that ever happen to you?

On one of those mornings, as I lay in bed with my eyes closed, not ready to start my day, a memory came to me. It was from quite a few years ago. I was in a workshop learning more about how to better connect with our intuition. That day we closed our eyes and imagined how far we could hear—how far we could see.

Back to my quiet morning. Imagining how far I could hear in those moments led my thoughts to meander even farther, until I had this piece I'd like to share with you today.

My hope is that it will be a reminder of the importance of connecting with nature, our Earth, the universe, and most importantly, yourself.

How far can you hear?

Can you hear . . .

The warmth of the sun

The protection of clouds

The guidance of stars

The pull of the moon

The cleansing of the sea

The whisper of wind

The emotions of rain

The wonder of snow

The force of storms

The pause of winter

The life of summer

The growth of spring

The release of fall

The love of Mother Earth

The promise of sunrise

The peace of sunset

The calm of morning

The stillness of night

The strength of trees

The joy of birds

The compassion of flowers

The innocence of animals
The majesty of mountains
The magic of words
The healing of touch
The vibration of energy
The call of desire
The voice of angels
The connection of souls
The oneness of source
The knowing of your heart
The heaviness of hate
The freedom of love
Can you hear them?
No?
Then, my child, it's time to be still and listen more closely.

Take action: If this resonated with you, download your free How Far Can You Hear? Bookmark and PDF by joining Laura Muirhead's newsletter. Stay connected and be the first to receive insights, inspiration, and exclusive updates!

Part 6

LIVING THE QUEEN CODE

(Themes: integration, clarity, sovereignty)

Chapter 25
BEING STILL TO MOVE FORWARD.
(THE SAGE)

Take a nap . . . then straighten your crown!

How often do you hear people saying: *keep hustling, keep creating, don't stop, move toward your goal?* And when you *do* stop, do you feel guilty? Guilty that you're not "moving forward," creating the next thing, or sliding your game piece to the next square?

Do you tell yourself that you're being lazy if you take a day (or more) off from the hamster wheel?

I hear it often, "I'm just having a lazy morning." It's not lazy to take a breath, to allow yourself to rest, to listen to your body. In fact, it can be just the opposite.

When we stop to give ourselves the space to rest, it allows our energy to rest and to align with the universe. It allows space for imagination, creativity, and for ideas to flow.

How can you create your next best thing if you aren't

tapping into all of that . . . all of your magic?

Some of the greatest inventors, when "stuck", would take a nap. Albert Einstein is one of them. Naps supposedly helped him with creativity and to focus better. It's said that he would doze off in a chair, holding a spoon above a metal plate. When the spoon would fall out of his hand, it would wake him up. Thomas Edison, Frank Lloyd Wright, and even Leonardo Da Vinci were fans of the power nap. I think so many adults dismiss the idea of a nice afternoon nap, considering it something for children. I say, if it's good enough for the greatest thinkers and creators, it's good enough for any of us and worth a try!

"A calm and modest life brings more happiness than the pursuit of success combined with constant restlessness."

– Albert Einstein

I've heard many entrepreneurs share stories of sales rolling in when they are away on vacation. Their phones happily chiming away while they lounge by the pool or on a beach, completely unplugged.

Taking time to reset is so important!

I've found that traveling or spending a few days reconnecting with friends can be just what my soul needs. It feels so good to reconnect with those who know you best, sharing stories and laughing.

It's necessary to take the time to refill our cups because if we don't, we will have nothing to pour from them into our own projects, clients, or customers.

I've noticed this again and again . . . people keep pushing through busy times, going nonstop. When they finally take a pause, they get sick. Their bodies crash with a cold or the flu. To me, it's their body telling them it's just had too much. It forces them to slow down. What if, instead, we learned to pause before it gets to that point?

An important part of setting personal policies for your Queen Code Mastery™ is self-care. Listening to the needs of your body and energy is part of that.

After I've been with a group of people for a few days, I know that I will need to take time for my energy to rest. Not everyone feels that need, but many do. Take the time, allow yourself the stillness to come back to yourself, and recharge.

This is my challenge to you, especially when you find yourself frustrated or feeling like you are spinning your wheels: Take a nap, a walk, a vacation, get a massage, or even a coffee or tea break.

Allow the stillness in, and notice what results you receive as you move forward with renewed energy.

Chapter 26
FROM EXCUSES TO EMPOWERMENT (THE ORACLE). THE AUTHORITY (OWNING CHOICES)

One important thing that I've learned is that if you are going to rule your Queendom fairly—in alignment, with clarity, and peace—is that you will have to let go of excuses.

You know, the ones that sound reasonable but keep you from moving forward.

See if you recognize any of these stories you might be telling yourself:

- "I'm stuck in place with no way to grow or have more abundance." (The Villager)
- "I've been hurt so many times, I can't trust anyone" (The Knight)
- "I just want everyone to be happy, but I'm exhausted and have to do everything myself." (The Servant)

- "Life should be perfect, but it isn't. It's just not fair, but it's because of everyone else." (The Princess)
- "I'm so angry - nothing in my world is working out. Why even bother trying to make things better?" (The Queen)
- "I feel lost and could really use some guidance; I just can't connect to anything." (The Inner Sorceress)

Believe it or not, we can tell ourselves anything we want . . . and we will believe it! Whether it's a true story or not. Often, we do it to protect ourselves, or at least that's what we believe we are doing. Sometimes these stories will end up keeping us upset or angry.

Let me give you an example.

I have a friend who loves to joke and poke a little fun. It's "just words" and is usually taken by their other friends in the joking way that it is intended.

One time, my friend said something in jest that didn't sit right with their friend. In fact, their friend was offended by the comment.

For weeks, their friend stewed about the comment, playing it over and over in their head. *Why would my friend say that about me? I thought they were supportive of me. I thought they cared about me. I thought we had a special bond. I thought they loved me.*

In the meantime, my friend—the supposed offending party—had no idea this was going on. They always joke around and, again, it's usually taken all in good fun.

Finally, a text was sent, saying how the friend was feeling. Saying that it has been a long time coming . . . sharing all that they were holding inside.

And guess what? My friend was surprised by the text. They felt awful, never intending for their offhanded comment to be taken the way it was. They didn't even remember making the comment. So many times, they had joked around, and it was always met with back-and-forth banter between friends.

This is exactly how we step out of our own power by telling a story to ourselves. One friend was making themselves miserable, believing a story that wasn't true. It wasn't a personal attack; it was simply a joke. What really happened was that their own insecurities got mirrored back, creating a story that kept them stuck.

And here's the truth: those same kinds of stories show up in our Queendoms too. The beauty is that they can be reframed into truths that support our goals and create a life filled with more clarity, happiness, and abundance.

Take a look at the excuses we often repeat and how they can be transformed into empowered truths:

- The Villager may say, *"I'm stuck in place with no way to grow or have more abundance."*
- The empowered truth: *"I always have choices. Even one small step today opens the door to new possibilities."*
- The Knight may hold the story, *"I've been hurt so many times, I can't trust anyone."*

- The empowered truth: *"My past does not define my future. I can set boundaries, protect myself, and still welcome healthy connections."*
- The Servant often says, *"I just want everyone to be happy, but I'm exhausted and have to do everything myself."*
- The empowered truth: *"I serve best when I am nourished. Asking for help and setting limits honors both me and those I love."*
- The Princess laments, *"Life should be perfect, but it isn't. It's just not fair, but it's because of everyone else."*
- The empowered truth: *"Life doesn't have to be perfect to be beautiful. I hold the power to create joy, even in imperfect circumstances."*
- The Queen in shadow might cry out, *"I'm so angry—nothing in my world is working out. Why even bother trying to make things better?"*
- The empowered truth: *"I can transform my anger into action. I have the authority to shift what is within my control and lead myself forward."*
- The Inner Sorceress whispers, *"I feel lost and could really use some guidance; I just can't connect to anything."*
- The empowered truth: *"My intuition is always available when I choose to listen. I trust the wisdom within me to guide my next step."*

This is the shift from excuses to empowerment. Each time you recognize the story you've been repeating, you can choose a new one.

There is no way to move into your authentic power while piling on excuses and telling stories. We can only hold one thought at a time. Similar to a light switch, it's either on or off, it's either a positive or negative thought. Choose intentionally. Take responsibility for how you want to show up.

The beauty of exploring the stories that may be playing out in our lives is that the unaligned stories can be reframed to aligned stories that support your goals, and create a life filled with more clarity, happiness, and abundance.

All the excuses weaken a Queen's authority. People in the Queendom see it whether the Queen does or not. Let's ditch the excuse pile, clear the decks, and reclaim your rightful place as ruler of your Queendom . . . where your choices, not your excuses, shape the crown you wear.

Chapter 27
FAMILY & LEGACY THREADS. THE WEAVER (INTEGRATING STORIES)

For years I knew I wanted to write a book, to tell my story. To tell the truth. But the arguments with myself were real. It wasn't just my story. It included, and would possibly affect, other family members.

I even had the title, *A Funny Thing Happened on the Way to My Life*. That came to me more than a decade ago when reflecting on the events of my life. And that was well before some of the big ones played out, like our house fire.

Once, when I told my friend about my hesitation to write my story, she said, "Well, maybe in the end you'll decide not to write it." I knew at that moment that I *would* write it, and I told her so.

Before I put the words on paper, I felt like a liar, like I was betraying myself and my truth. This goes against my own core values, some of them being authenticity, truth, and individuality.

Then why was I struggling to put my story out into the world?

A big reason was a story I told myself—that I was protecting others. I was worried about what family members would think when the truth came out. Would there be fallout? Would they even believe me?

Because, when one person's story has been told for so long, told to others as fact, when that story is challenged, it can have unexpected consequences. Maybe the truth won't even be believed. Maybe people will be angry that the truth has been told with the potential of "pulling out the rug" from under the original storyteller.

And I wasn't a writer anyway.

Each of these potential outcomes played over and over in my mind. My intention wasn't to hurt anyone or their reputation. It was for me to be honest with myself, be true to myself and what I know.

A huge shift for me came with finding the right mentor to walk along with me in writing and publishing my book. There's a saying about borrowing someone else's belief in you until you can believe it for yourself. I found this to be true for me in this journey.

The people you surround yourself with are so important, and I found that, especially in my author journey, the confidence and support that my publisher, Karen Weaver, offered made all the difference.

Eventually, I've come to see that writing my book wasn't just about sharing my story with the world—it was about healing. Putting the words on paper gave me clarity. It was less about convincing anyone else, and more about finally being honest with myself.

A huge shift came in the pinch me moment of standing in front of a Times Square billboard that revealed the cover of my book. It was a dream that I never knew I had come true.

Of course it was a celebration, but it was also a moment of confidence and confirmation. My story was going to be out in the world and there was no going back. It was time to roll with it.

Family stories are complicated. They're woven together over years, sometimes generations, and everyone remembers them a little differently. Writing mine didn't erase anyone else's; it simply gave me space to honor my own.

It didn't matter anymore who read it . . . if family members read it. Of course I want people to read it, to be inspired and connect to the stories, but more importantly, I was now free. Free from doubt, free from feeling self-betrayal, free from feeling unauthentic.

And—spoiler alert—none of my what-ifs have happened. Instead, I've received beautiful feedback from people who have read and loved my book. It has traveled the world with me, and it has been nominated for and won awards.

Writing my book became an act of sovereignty. It was my

way of claiming the crown in my own life, of saying: I will no longer let someone else's version of the story define me. Choosing to put my words on paper, to release them into the world, was one of the ways I honor my personal policies and Queen Code Mastery™.

At its heart, Queen Code Mastery™ is about self-leadership. It's about choosing alignment over approval, truth over silence, and authenticity over the weight of someone else's expectations. My memoir isn't just a story, it's a declaration. A reminder to myself, and to anyone reading it, that your story matters and you are the only one who can tell it.

My story, like everyone's, is full of twists and turns I never saw coming—a house fire, incredible opportunities, unexpected challenges, some things I wouldn't have chosen—but that shaped me all the same. Over time, I've learned to meet those plot twists with curiosity. Instead of asking, "Why me?" I ask, "What's here for me?" That shift, seeing the opportunity, reframing the experience, finding gratitude in the moment, is what has allowed me to grow instead of remaining stuck.

Looking back, I can see how every detour in my own life held a gift. Each experience, no matter how painful or surprising, offered wisdom I wouldn't trade. And that's what I carry forward; not just the story itself, but in the realization that even the most unexpected turns can lead you to exactly where you're meant to be.

And that's why I know the journey doesn't end with a single book; it keeps unfolding. Putting my memoir out in the world is just the beginning, as my author journey continues to open doors I never expected to stand in front of. That's the magic of owning your story: it frees you, heals you, and shapes the legacy you leave behind.

Final Chapter
QUEEN CODE MASTERY™ IN ACTION. THE QUEEN (RETURNING TO SOVEREIGNTY, FULL CIRCLE)

When I created Queen Code Mastery™ I never imagined that one day I would be staying in a castle. Yet that's exactly where I found myself. Not just any castle, but an Irish castle, on an island, surrounded by centuries of history and beauty, with my room overlooking the water. And I wasn't just visiting. I was there as a bestselling author and an international speaker.

Talk about a pinch me moment.

Not long ago, this kind of experience would've felt like a dream way out of reach. Something for someone else. Someone more polished, more accomplished, more "qualified." But here's the funny thing about expansion: when it finally arrives, it often feels surprisingly natural, like slipping into a place you've belonged all along.

The thing is, I was never meant to be a writer. In my

family, that position was meant for someone else. I definitely never saw myself speaking in front of a room full of people, on a stage in London, my first speaking experience, or in a castle in Ireland.

Sure, I had taken a speech class in high school . . . only because it was mandatory. But it was not something I was a fan of, and I struggled to even find a topic.

How was it even possible for that same girl to be comfortable in a room full of other authors, standing in front of an audience to speak?

That day in the castle, for a split second, I felt the weight of it: *You're about to speak in a castle*. And then, just as quickly, something else . . . Ease. Comfort. As if the castle itself whispered, *You belong here.*

My steps echoed on the stone floor, and I couldn't help thinking, "Well, this is definitely not high school speech class anymore." My room overlooked the water, and I'd wake up each morning to mist rising over the lake, a view that felt like it belonged in a storybook. And yes, there was even a butler who made sure everything was in place. Can you imagine? A girl who once dreaded high school speech class now being served tea in an Irish castle before standing on stage as an international speaker.

That's how expansion feels.

That day, I didn't feel like an imposter. I felt at home. My spirit felt like it had walked these halls long before my feet ever did. It was familiar, as if I was stepping into a dream that had simply been waiting for me to catch up.

It didn't just happen though. It began when I committed to writing my memoir, *A Funny Thing Happened on the Way to My Life*. Once I agreed to tell my story, to share my truth and my *authentic self*, magical things began to unfold.

My face and book on a Times Square billboard.

Global speaking opportunities.

Achieving awards for my writing and work.

Magazine covers and articles.

Collaborative author opportunities.

International travel.

It felt like a snowball effect: one aligned "yes" leading to the next, each step opening the door to another. And all of that unfolded in less than a year.

None of this was forced. It all came from saying "yes" to what felt aligned, one step at a time.

That's how creativity works. It carries us from a dream to a doorway, from longing to living. When I first had the idea for Queen Code Mastery™, it was just that, an idea. A whisper. I could have brushed it off, told myself no one would care, that it was impractical. But I didn't. I followed the nudge. I let myself imagine what it could become. And imagination is what opened the doors.

The framework of Queen Code Mastery™ helps hold your vision steady when doubts creep in, and it keeps you moving when fear wants you to stand still.

The castle, for me, was a mirror of that expansion. Not

because I needed stone walls or chandeliers to validate me, but because it reflected the woman I had become, the woman who once thought she wasn't ready and realized she had been ready all along.

And it made me wonder: how many times do we all sell ourselves short with a story of limitation?

"That's not for me."

"People like me don't get to do that."

"Maybe someday..."

But what if your "someday" is closer than you think? What if the castle you've been dreaming of is simply the very next step?

So let me ask you: What is your castle? At what point are you telling yourself it's too far away? And how would it feel to finally stand inside it, realizing it fits you perfectly?

Here's the truth: the castle isn't the ending. It's not the finish line wrapped up with a ribbon. It's a doorway. A beginning. A reminder that expansion is never one-and-done, it's always unfolding.

Queen Code Mastery™ brought me to an island castle as an author and a speaker. But that isn't the end of the story. It's just one of the doorways. There's so much more to come, and it's already in motion. I'm not exactly sure where it will lead, but I'm up for the journey.

And the same is true for you. Wherever you are right now, whatever dream you've been holding onto, know this: your castle is closer than you think. And when you finally step into it, you'll find it feels less like a miracle and more like the most natural next step in who you were always becoming.

Castles aren't just built of stone, they're built of choices, one brick at a time. And so is your expansion.

THE PEARL PRINCIPLE
(FROM AWAKENED MAGAZINE)

Lately I've been thinking about oysters and Sir Isaac Newton.

And not because I'm hungry or brushing up on high school science.

You may be asking, *"What actually is going on in her mind?"*

Stay with me on this.

When something gets stuck in an oyster - sand, a piece of shell, an irritant - the oyster reacts by coating it with layers of nacre, we know it as mother of pearl.

Those layers become like a cushion that absorbs shock, resists cracks, and adds toughness. They shimmer with luster when the light hits just right. And this process isn't quick. Sometimes it takes up to four years.

What results is a pearl.

Interesting, for sure, but what about Sir Isaac Newton, you ask?

Newton gave us laws of physics. His third law of motion is: *"Every action has an equal and opposite reaction."*

You see it when a bird flies, a fish swims, a car drives, or a rocket launches. Even when you lean on a wall, the wall leans back with equal force.

So, what does that have to do with oysters?

Here's where I'll take some scientific leeway (or maybe not). What if the oyster's reaction to the irritant follows Newton's law…the bigger the irritant, the bigger the pearl?

I don't know if that's *technically* true, but it makes perfect sense when you consider it in this context.

Now…let's apply that to our lives.

As we move through the journey of life, we come across challenges, plot twists, and yes, even irritants. What if we thought of those as our grains of sand?

What if, instead of fighting them, we layered over them with learning, growth, and resilience - allowing something unexpectedly beautiful to form? Something we never could have imagined.

And in the end, we don't just have challenges. We have pearls.

I've seen this in my own life, and as I share in my memoir *A Funny Thing Happened on the Way to My Life*, this has happened time and again.

The fire that burned our house down opened the door to the home we now love, and even to a second house. That led me to explore working with clay, making ceramics, and eventually opening my own pottery and art studio when circumstances shifted and became uncomfortable. And childhood challenges? They shaped my independence, nudged me to graduate high school early, and eventually led me across the country to grow on my own.

Just like the distance an arrow flies is dependent on how far the bow is pulled back, and where it hits depends on the aim, I suggest that the size of the challenge is related to the size of the resulting pearl.

I've witnessed this in my life.

After years of holding back, arguing with myself about writing my memoir and sharing my stories, when I finally allowed it to go out into the world, amazing opportunities were placed in my path.

It was as if the arrow had been pulled all the way back. The trajectory was incredible.

It started with a Times Square billboard, then speaking on global stages, international business and book awards… and a movie. Of course all of that involved travel to cities and countries I had not previously visited. England, Dublin, and Australia. Not to mention an Irish castle…

The largest, most beautiful pearl!

Even the exciting milestones, a new school, a job, a marriage, children, stepping into business ventures, came wrapped in their own challenges.

But each one? Every bit of grit, growth, and learning? Another pearl. Together they've become a string of pearls I never could have imagined, tough, luminous, and uniquely mine. A string of life pearls.

What about you?

Can you look back and see your pearls? Can you add today's grit, today's challenge, today's opportunity to that incredible string you're creating?

Maybe Newton was right and his law does apply to life: every challenge really does create an equal and opposite reaction - the chance to grow a pearl.

Laura Muirhead is an internationally acclaimed author, accomplished artist and the CFO of her family's multimillion-dollar company. She is also the creator of Queen Code Mastery™ program and the Queen Code Oracle Card Deck, which guide multi-passionate women to find clarity, set boundaries and elevate both life and business, stepping into their full potential. Laura's work bridges creativity and business, demonstrating that success can be achieved on both sides of the spectrum.

Her personal journey is as dynamic as her professional life – she is a licensed pilot, an energy healer, and the author of *A Funny Thing Happened on the Way to My Life*, as well as a beloved children's book and three journals. Laura's life story is one of resilience and reinvention. From navigating the unexpected twists of life to rebuilding after a devastating house fire, she draws inspiration from her experiences to empower others.

Laura enjoys photography and exploring the world. She

splits her time between homes in New Jersey and Michigan. Laura cherishes time with her husband, grown children, close friends, Labrador retriever and a life filled with creativity and adventure.

lauramuirhead.com

www.ingramcontent.com/pod-product-compliance
Lightning Source LLC
Chambersburg PA
CBHW031253290426
44109CB00012B/556